TWO GIRLS STARING AT THE CEILING

TWO GIRLS STARING AT THE CEILING   LUCY FRANK

schwartz & wade books · new york

All rights reserved. Published in the United States by Schwartz & Wade Books, an imprint of Random House Children's Books, a division of Random House LLC, a Penguin Random House Company, New York.

The following poems were originally published on worldvoices.pen.org/two-girls-staring in different form: "Bedpan"; "Morning Is the Time to Sleep"; "And In the Silence" as "And Suddenly"; "Smiley-Face Balloons" as "So Far from How"; "'Let's Talk About Happy Things'" as "Mom"; and "Forget" as "Not Me."

Schwartz & Wade Books and the colophon are trademarks of Random House LLC.

Visit us on the Web! randomhouse.com/teens
Educators and librarians, for a variety of teaching tools,
visit us at RHTeachersLibrarians.com

Library of Congress Cataloging-in-Publication Data
Frank, Lucy.
Two girls staring at the ceiling / Lucy Frank.—First edition.
pages cm
Summary: In this novel in verse, two very different girls bond while hospitalized for Crohn's disease.
ISBN 978-0-307-97974-2 (hardcover)—ISBN 978-0-307-97975-9 (glb)
ISBN 978-0-307-97976-6 (ebook)
[1. Novels in verse. 2. Crohn's disease—Fiction. 3. Hospitals—Fiction.
4. Friendship—Fiction.] I. Title.
PZ7.5.F73 Tw 2014
[Fic]—dc23
2013023236

The text of this book is set in 10.5-point Aaux Pro.
Book design by Rachael Cole

Printed in the United States of America
10 9 8 7 6 5 4 3 2 1
First Edition

For Peter, again, as always

HOW TO READ THIS BOOK

In this book, you will see a line down the center of many pages, which represents the curtain that separates the hospital beds of the main character, Chess (on the left), and her roommate, Shannon. The two girls talk to each other, mostly through the curtain. When the curtain is open or Chess is no longer in the room, the line disappears.

The text should be read across the line, rather than as separate columns.

ER

The faces on the pain chart
wear numbered bow ties.
Zero has a dimwit smile.
Ten's eyes trickle tears.

"Put ten. They'll take us faster."
Mom's face
would be off the chart
if they measured fear.

A gray-faced woman cradles
her belly. A cougher fights
to catch his breath.
A baby screams.

What number?
Four Face is like: Um, is there a bathroom here?
Six ate a rancid clam.
Eight's ice cream fell off his cone.

"Big as a grapefruit by the time
they found it," whispers the lady beside us.
"And we're not talking
the three-for-a-dollar kind."

"Ow! Owww!"
a girl's voice behind us wails.
"Owwwwww! This is getting
really bad!"

What number? Higher?
So they'll take us sooner? Lower?
So I can be sure
they'll let me go?

"Hey!" the girl yells.
"I'm in pain here, people!
I been sitting in this chair
since two a.m.

"And don't be pretending
you don't know me!
I saw that *Oh shit it's Shannon* look
before you went all blank and bland and shit!"

The gray-faced woman groans.
The baby thrashes in its mother's arms.
Everyone moves farther
from the coughing man.

"Chess, sweetie. Let me do the paperwork."
Mom's cuticle is bleeding.
If I say five,
will they let me go?

"And don't give me some little med student!
The last guy swore
those pills would work,
and look at me!"

If we don't look, will the girl stop screaming?
Not even six a.m. I dressed for work.
If they take me next,
I might not be late.

"Yo! I'm a walking pain chart,
if I could even walk,
which I'm in too much pain,
which you would see

if you'd take the fuckin' time
to fuckin' LOOKIT ME!"

The old lady holding
the girl's hand sees Mom wince,
throws her a mortified,
scared sigh.

Paid today.
Birthday next week.
Boston trip
to look at colleges.

They could say
it was a freak, a fluke,
too much hot sauce, too many pickles,
mixing marshmallows with beer.

"Francesca Goodman?
Vomiting, diarrhea, passing blood?"
asks the nurse who takes my blood,
my temp, my pulse.

Or the thousands of raspberries I've been eating.
Eight and a half?
Fourteen?
Ninety-three?

"Is it a dull ache? A burning, stabbing,
cramping, searing pain?
When did it start?
Is it constant or does it come and go?"

If I don't tell
anyone,
I can forget
it happened.

If I can forget
it happened,
I'll never
have to tell.

"How're you doing, Francesca?"
The doctor's face so kind
I almost cry.
"Not too good," I say.

"Yo! You better save me, Doc!
Cuz your ugly face
is not gonna be the last thing
on this earth I see!"

The spindle-limbed, stub-haired girl
cuts dragon eyes at me—
"Who the fuck you lookin' at?"—
before we're both wheeled away.

Green scrubs blue scrubs white coats
push park poke
ID band IV tube
toss terms
start with *C* end w/ *scopy*

CT

catheterize

  colon

      chronic

conservative

  clinical

      corticosteroids

  colonoscopy

"Excuse me. Did you say steroids?
Because my performance could use
a little enhancement these days."

Monitor Me, floating somewhere
near the ceiling, hears my voice,
too shrill, too chipper,

As peering docs
see no Me,
just belly.

"I'm a runner, you know."

With legs lovely
as an antelope,
he said.

"I don't want big ugly bulgy muscles, though.
Will this kind of steroids give me—"

"Don't worry," says the doc, whose shaved
head shimmers in the fluorescent light.
"Those are anabolic steroids.
This is a different drug entirely
to suppress inflammamma . . .
high dose shortest possible
to minimimimize . . .

"Okay then, Mom.
It's best if you step out now.
So, Francesca, we're just
going to insert a little tube—"

Monitor Me says run,
run fast,
run now.

Then   somehow
makes me find my mom
a smile.

With her last small wave
as the door closes,

Even the wings
David drew

On my hand around
his number

Seem
to fade.

"Relax   try to relax   just relax.
Don't worry. I have a special trick
to make it slide
down easy does it
that's a good girl
swallow swallow sip and swallow
relax it will be much easier
if you—

"Hold her arms for me,
will you, please, Linda."

I beg fight beg
for breath fight
gag choke drown
as he wiggles
stuffs bores
the tube
in
up
down
my nose

Invades
me
deeper
deeper. . . .

Jump back
to the French café,
where just last week
the scary-smart alumna lady
said you were so bright, so poised,
impressively well prepared.

Skip past
the latte making you feel
like a woodpecker was drilling
through your stomach,
the almond croissant
you knew was not a good idea.

Forget
days curled
on the nurse's cot,
nights hunched
on the bathroom floor.

Conjure
the sweet tang
of raspberries,
tanned arms,
dark eyes,
hair streaked
all goldy by the sun.

Flash
to Bri and Lexie
and that flushed, fizzy,
laughing-at-nothing,
something's-about-
to-happen feeling:

*"Chess, what's up
with the sudden
interest in produce?"*

"It's not the produce
she's interested in.
It's the meat!"

"Shut up, Lexie!
Don't look now, Chess!
He's oogling you
the way you oogle
his raspberries."

"It's ogle, not oogle."

"Uh-uh. The way Chess does it,
it's a definite oogle."

"Chess, how many trips
to the farm stand
are we gonna have to make
before you say hi?"

"Chess! It's Berry Boy!
Mr. Sugar Snap!
What's he doing at this party?"

"Don't call him that!"

"Then go ask him his name.
Look at him there, all alone
with his guitar."

"Chess. Remember
the Plan."

"Aren't you glad now
I loaned you my dress?"

"You ask him, Bri."

"Me? Chess,
I'm not the one
he thinks is hot."

"See? That wasn't so bad, was it?
Your throat might feel a little sore
till you get used to it."

The doctor tapes the tube
to my nose.
Tells me what a good girl I am.

Deep blue, with silver stars, the longest nails I've ever seen run the elevator. Whatever this pain stuff is, it's working great. "I love your nails," I think I say. "Thought you was supposed to be off," says green jacket pushing my bed. Nail lady snorts, presses B. Cab-drivered through a bed traffic jam, IV bags dangle squiddish in the chilly light. "Could I get another blanket, please?" Wheeled into dim room with fun-house tunnel. Offloaded. Need to pee. Through whirring murk: "How's moo shu sound? I could go for a little moo shu pork today." "Excuse me, is there a restroom I could use first? And another blanket would be good." "Thought you're on a diet, Kenny. Plus, Tiny wants Chinese." "Tiny always wants Chinese. We had Chinese yesterday." "How you doing, hon? Hangin' in? We'll have you out quick as we can. Speaking of diet, d'you hear Kimberly's expecting? And you said she was just packing on the pounds. Hold your breath now, sweetheart. Don't breathe. Okay. Breathe."
Not easy with this tube clogging my nose,
filling my throat. "Do you see anything?
Can you tell me what's wrong with me?
Is it something you die of?"
Why don't they hear me?
"Almost done now,
don't worry. Kenny,
we haven't had Italian
in a while. How 'bout
some pasta? Okay!
Last one, hon!
Doin' good!
Big breath
now.

Hold
your
breath.

Okay.

Breathe."

Smiley-face balloons
ask how I am
not too bad
except my teeth
weigh too much
to move my mouth
this bed's a raft
floating so far
from *who* I am
my head can't grab
onto the *how.*

One good thing:
if I die,
and David tells,
I'll never know.

FIRST DAY

Wheeled into a fluorescent world of two
TVs on brackets, two nightstands, tray tables,
wall panels bristling with gizmos, wires,
monitors above two vacancies
where beds should be.

No, wait.
Green curtains hide a third
bed farthest from the door.
Who's moaning
on the other side?

I'll take the spot closest to the door,
by the bathroom, I try to say.
But before my tongue's organized
organized, my bed's pushed
into the middle,

Up against those
cream-of-pea-green
lima-bean-green
Nile-bile-algae-vile
slimy-toxic-waste-green curtains.

And curtains close
around me, too.

Good morning afternoon good evening
how we doing time
to check your temp your pressure your
IV take you for that test
get some blood
hang a new IV
sweetheart
cookie
lovey
honey
mi amor.

Meanwhile,
one by one,
gross green bubbles
glub up from my insides,
slip down the tube.

Bedpan:
Let's
not
go
there.

"Let's talk about happy things,"
Mom says.
"Like that pistachio ice cream
with the cherries we always get
at Moon Palace for your birthday,
not that I'm saying that's where
we should go. Plus from what the doctor's
telling me, you probably shouldn't eat
the nuts anymore, or the cherries,
or ice cream, for that matter.
We should pick someplace special
this year.
I mean, I can't believe you'll still
be in the hospital next week,
though if you are . . . I mean . . .
we'll just . . . bring the party here.

"You hear me? Chess?
Chessie?"

Pour of moon on water, sting of breeze,
soft sway of waves rock rocking us.

Who wouldn't fall
for a boy

Who adds, "And that was antelope,
not cantaloupe."

Who says, "Even in the dark
you have the brightest eyes."

Says it like he's never even thought
those words about a girl.

Was it just last night,
that throbbing party
lit with lanterns?
That pine tree
where he strummed
Spanishy melodies
so haunting
I forgot the pain
chewing through my belly as
we walked into the shadows
till we heard the water,
and David said, "Whoa! Did you see
those wings? Bet you anything
it's an owl!" And in a thrum
of tree frogs we followed
the flash of white
through a Queen Anne's lace–y
meadow to a fence,
his hands fizzed my skin
as he lifted me over, we tiptoed
past one sleeping house,
another, to the rocks sloping
to the water's edge,
untied the canoe,
kicked off flip-flops. . . .

    "Yeah, no

drove her up to Albany

             like four a.m.

    Room five sixteen."

Mom's voice
floats in,
drifts out again.

        "Yeah, no

     out of the blue

so healthy

     no, no I know   all that weight

        but I assumed

I mean

     we ran together

almost

        every day   not that I

     lost a single . . ."

I fight to keep her words
from gibbering,

My mind
from jumbling.

     "I know

        like best friends

nothing

      she doesn't tell me . . ."

"Mom?
What are you doing?"

"Just making a few phone calls.
I already sent out an email
letting everyone know."

"Know what?
Mom. You're not . . ."

Each word
the tube rasps
my throat.

"Brianna's mom said Bri and Lexie
have been so worried
they can't reach you,
wondering what happened."

The weight
of the unspoken
presses me deeper
in the bed.

"Mom, you're not saying
anything to anyone, not telling
them to come here, right?
Please! Just tell them
I'll be fine!"

And I can't tell if this buzzy jigging
as I stare at the cellulite-dimpled squares
on the ceiling is drip-dripping steroids
rip-roaring to the rescue
this kind of steroids makes people weird
that young nice nurse said
almost everyone gets fat

"Oh look how cute
with those round cheeks
Chubby Chessie Chess the Chunk
Don't listen to them, sweetie. You—
Right, Mom. I have a beautiful face.
You do. You just happen
to have gotten my genes.
Yeah. Size 14!
What? Chessie, I was never a 14!
And you were never bigger
than a 10!"

Please, God,
don't let me get fat again
just when I thought
I knew
this body
I've trained
toned
scrutinized
compared

So sure
I could caffeinate
sleep Advilize
sweet-talk muscle

mind over matter
this body I thought
I mostly
almost liked
or at least
didn't totally
loathe.

And for those hours
minutes
last night
oh . . .

"Shhh. Try to relax, sweetie.
Let the medicine do its job."

Was it just
last night
David said,
"Would you be sad
if our owl turned out
to be a seagull?"
as we slid the boat
into the lake and rowed
to an island that turned out
to be a rock barely
big enough for two?

Said: "Uh . . . how're
we gonna get back
from here?" as we watched
the boat drift off
into the water lilies?

Said: "Do we care?
Maybe, but not now, right?"

Said he wished
he had his guitar
so he had something
to do with his hands?

Then we both talked
too much, too fast,
to talk away
the awkwardness,

Pointed out
bogus constellations,

agreed we're so not
party people,
only came, in fact,
because his dad lives
just down the road,
and my friends
decided we needed
to get out more,

And I told him
I wished I could
drive a tractor
and sell raspberries
all summer,
not plug numbers
into a spreadsheet
at Mom's ex-boyfriend's
accounting firm,

And my mind leaped
with summer things
we'd do together,
and though the breeze
smelled like rain,
the rock was rough and pointy,
and the bugs were biting,
I couldn't imagine ever
being sad again.

And by the time the thumping bass beats
from the party faded and lights winked out
around the lake, pain nibbled
at my belly, but his hands

let me forget,
we warmed each other
against the night,
and if the owl flew by,
my eyes were too melted
with his kisses
to see.

And when he said:
"I can't think of anything to say
that isn't totally corny,"
I'd have answered
"Say it anyway,"

Except a boa constrictor
was squeezing my breath away
a shark was ripping
my insides,

And I tried so hard
to hold on
not let him see
not let him know
not stop
not spoil
hold on.

"**S**hould have taken her to the doctor

    weeks ago

        kept her home last night,

  said, you worked all day. And

        your stomach's killing you.

Said, whose party

      is this, anyway? Who

         do you even know

             in Hillsdale?

Made her

      tell me what happened.

I mean,

         no phone   no wallet

    no underpants?"

Under the covers
I hold my hand
as if it's his.

How bad
could I have been
if I remembered
we needed to go back
and get his guitar?

Skin white as the fat
on a leg of lamb,
white scarf over no hair,
eyelids waxy as a corpse . . .

Here in the night,
the only lights the flickering
fluorescence of her machines,
my call button's LED.

Her sheeted chest
flutters . . .
flutters . . .
doesn't.

"The lady in the bed by the window?"
I tell the intercom. "She was like twitching
and moaning before, but I think
she may have stopped breathing.

"No, no. I'm not out of bed.
But I can't seem to sleep,
so I've been watching
through the curtain.

"No. Wait! She just twitched again.
And cleared her throat.
Yeah. Yeah.
It's okay. She's okay!"

I let the curtain drop,
sink into the safety of my bed.
"Sorry to bother you. She's fine.

She's on the phone."

"Sam? Do you know where my shoes
and stockings are?"

Voice a scrape, a creak, a raven's croak:

"Sam, my cab's waiting!
No! They're not under the bed!
I looked!"

"Hello, Halberstam, it's me, Mrs. Klein.
I need you to come with the affidavit.
Tell Sam to bring the blue valise.
And the passport.

"Sam, it's me again.
I'm not supposed to be here, Sam.
Sammy, there's been some mistake.
Without the passport
they won't let me leave."

When I was little, keeping watch
in the night, counting cars
could sometimes keep away
the night beetles.

I watch the darkness,
listen to silence, until
a nurse's light glimmers
through the curtain:

"You sure you weren't dreaming, hon?
I never heard Mrs. Klein say a word."

When I was little,
waiting for the night to end,
my dad's flashlight was enough
to scare away the night beetles.

There are no lights here.
No sound but the bubbling hum
of her oxygen machine.
Nothing to count

but the glub
of the drain,
and the drugs
silently marching
down the tube
into my arm.

SECOND DAY

Morning is the time to sleep,
dreaming my old dreams:

Hot backseat love
with someone who turns out

To be Mr. Mooney, the custodian.
Why are the SATs in Chinese?

My cell's dropped in the toilet,
and it's ringing and I've lost my keys.

Welcoming those *Not that again!* dreams
like an old familiar *Seinfeld,*

While carts rattle, mops slap,
conversations filter in

Like sun striping
through the blinds.

Do I dream four frowning docs
in shower caps,

Young blue-scrubbed docs filing
in like a line of ducklings to gather
round my bed?

Could the "patient" person
they're talking about be me?

"You know, everyone's saying
what a great patient you are,"
Mom says as she unpacks
my pillow, socks, the afghan
Nana crocheted for me,

Plugs in my electric toothbrush,
stacks the as-yet-unopened books
from the AP English summer reading list
on the tray table beside my bed.

"I told them I'd expect nothing less.
Even when you were little,
when you got your shots,
it was me who cried,
even if I never let you see."

Sweet coffee kiss,
soft hiss of drawers
opening and closing,
rustle of papers.
My eyes haze.
I let her words blur
till

". . . told Bri you weren't
quite ready for her to go
get you raspberries but—"

"What? No! Mom! Don't
let her go there. And I can't
see anyone! Mom! No!
Tell her no!"

"Okay, sweetie.
Go back to sleep.
It's gonna take me an hour
to get to work.
I'd better go."

"Mommy, no!
Don't leave me!"

"You'll be fine.
And it will all be fine.
My strong, precious girl."

"Oy, so young!"

    "With all those tubes
    and not a word of complaint"

"I wonder what"

  "Peeked at her chart. It doesn't"

"Such a pretty name, Francesca."

    "Such a sweet face"

"But so skinny. *Vey iz mir.*"

No faces for the voices
till a green jacket man pushes my bed
toward the door and I see four stout ladies
in beauty-parlor-perfect wigs
and dresses too hot for July
spraddle-legged on the window seat
behind Mrs. Klein,
next to nectarines, cottage cheese,
hard-boiled eggs, pocketbooks.

The *tsk* chorus follows
as he wheels me past a boy
in an Ichabod Crane black
coat and hat, sleeping openmouthed
by the door.

"Where are they taking her?"

"Tests. Always more tests."

"Heshy! Move your chair so they can get through!"

"No need to raise your voice.
I understand, my love.
You're a little upset.
But now you're in your nice new
room, so let's just get you into bed,
okay, cookie?"

"You understand shit! I am not your love.
And I'm no damn Chips Ahoy!, either!
NO ONE puts their hands on me,
you GOT that, cookie?"

"I'm just trying to be nice."

"Do I look like I need nice?
What I NEED is for you to stop shuffling
me around like some kinda luggage.
Then I need you to leave
me the HELL alone.
Which goes for you, too,
whoever the hell you are.
You think I don't see you
peeping at me through the curtain?
WHAT? No one around here's
ever seen a bitch on steroids?"

I shrink into my covers,
let the clanging buzzing roaring
in my head drown her roars,
until the curtains part, and

IV pole tangled with tubes,
eyes almost swallowed

in her man-in-the-moon face,

the lollipop-head, dragon-eyed,
puff-bellied emergency room girl
flops down in my chair
and tucks up paper-slippered
feet too big
for her tiny body.

Says, "Hope you're not planning
on sleeping anytime soon. No way
I can sleep with all this shit
they got me on.
You're not a moaner, are you?
First room they had me in, the lady
whined and carried on all night."

Hair patchy, dry,
like doll hair cut
with kindergarten scissors.

"I used to be hot, if you can believe that.
Till they gave me the evil juice.
Saves your life and makes you wish
you were dead.
Know what I'm saying?"

Eyes too old for a girl
jump from the tube in my arm
to the bags on my IV pole.
She snorts a laugh.

"I guess you do.

Welcome to the club.
Not that I give a shit about being hot.
Hot's a pain in the ass. Not that you'd
know. Just joking. You're still looking
pretty good. How long you been in?
Hey! You're not closing your eyes?
Want some of my Jell-O, or an icey?
I scared that nurse so bad
she gave me three.
Oh, right. No food for you
with that NG tube.
They didn't dare stick one
down my nose this time.
How much evil juice
they pumping into you?"

"I don't know."

My voice floats in
from a distant galaxy.

"You didn't ask?"

A line of earrings studs one ear.
A cross dangles from the other.

"Act like a wimp, they tell you *nada.*
You know, you look like shit.
We should get the nurse."

"It's okay. I'm okay. Really.
I don't want to bother them."

I need her to understand this is not me,
this person lying here with patient hair
(back squashed flat,
top like rooster feathers)
two patient gowns
(one frontwards,
one backwards,
to keep the world
from my bare butt)

Even as the steroids rampaging
through my veins make my blood roar
as she glares her dragon glare.

"Hello! Nurse! There's a girl in here
could use some help!
Are we gonna get some help,
or do I need to come out there
and mess you up?"

"So an octopus
walks into a bar
and asks for a beer."
Poppy, too loud,
is laughing in advance
as the girl's voice booms
through the curtain.

"Yo. News flash, Doc!
You don't have to talk so slow.
I'm not five. Or stupid.
Just sick. Remember?

"Bet you remember the career advice
I gave you last time, too. How you
should be one of those coroner guys,
like on *CSI* and shit.

"I mean, if you're this bad
with people, do us all a favor.
Switch to corpses."

Nana bustles, fusses, reaches
for the clicker.
"Would you like to watch
a little TV, Cupcake?"

"Barb, I'm in the middle
of the joke! Unless
you've heard it, Chessie."

"Steve, it's not the dirty one?"

"No, Nana. It's fine."
I summon up a smile.
"I always like this one."

Nana, smelling of Chanel
smoothes back my hair.
"The earrings look just lovely!
I'm so glad we didn't
wait for your
birthday to— Oh, my goodness!
Is that a—
I don't know what you
call them these days.
In our day we called them hickeys."

"She's about to be seventeen
years old, Barb. You ask me,
it's high time she had a boyfriend.
Right, Chessie?"

On our island, David asks:
"So do you have a boyfriend?"
When I say, "No. Not really,"
he answers, "Awesome!"

And by moonlight
and the flashlight app
on my cell phone,
scribbles on my hand.

"How'm I FEELING, Doc?
'Bout time someone
in this shithole asked me that.

"How the HELL YOU THINK
I'M FEELING?"

"She's got some mouth on her,
that little girl. How old
do you think—"

"Nineteen, not that it's your business,
and I got ears, too, lady! And a name.
Shannon Elizabeth Williams. So
if you got something to say to me . . ."

"Okaaay! Here's
one you haven't heard."
Poppy's back in hearty mode.
"So what did Buddha
say to the hot dog vender?"

"OWWWW!"

"I haven't touched you yet!"

"Make me one with everything!"

"And you better not . . . OWWWW!"

"Why do you always have to give me
such a hard time?
Why can't you be more like
this nice little girl next to you?"

"You mean all meek and shit?"

"No, just pleasant.
She's not feeling any better
than you are, but she always
manages a thank-you and a smile."

"Cuz her evil juice
hasn't worked its magic yet.
Just wait. You'll see."

"What is she talking about,
evil juice?"

"What do you think's wrong
with that little girl? I understand
she's upset, but rude like that?
There's no excuse—"

"Frankly, I'm more worried
about Chessie. How're you doing, there,
Cupcake? You've been awfully quiet."
Poppy leans in for a kiss.

"Anything we can get you before we go?"
Or bring next time?"

"I'm fine," I tell them,
telling myself the lump
clogging my throat
is just the tube.

"I promise. I'll be fine."

"**K**nock, knock!
We were here to see Jared's
dermatologist, so
we thought we'd pop in
and say hi."

"Ma, I think she's sleeping,"
Jared whispers.

Jared from the sandbox,
from the school bus,
Jared destined to be valedictorian,
whose dad is our dentist,
who Mom, I know, wishes
was my boyfriend,
who before—No! Don't
let yourself even
think of David—
my friends swore
I was doomed
to marry, saying,
the good news is,
you'll get free dental care.

"Ma, come on," says Jared.
"Let's just go."

And even through closed eyes
I can see how I must look to him.

"I just want to say one thing.
Chessie, honey," says Mrs. Kaye.
"A girl at work has what your mom said
you might have, and as long as she avoids

stress and gets plenty of rest,
she's fine."

I squeeze my eyes tighter.
Wait for them to go away.

"**S**o, the immune system
as I'm sure you know,
protects the body
from viruses, bacteria and other . . ."

She's so cool, this doctor
in the orange Crocs,
with the glasses I'd get
if I needed glasses,
corkscrew hair
miraculously pinned up
with a pencil,

". . . foreign organisms.
Sometimes, however,
the cells supposed to fight enemies
can turn on your own body.
We call this . . ."

Talking to me like
I'm just as cool,
as smart. I wonder
if my hair's curly enough
to curl like that. I love
her engagement ring,
so not flashy, yet
so sparkly. I wonder

". . . autoimmunity.
Researchers think certain bacteria,
viruses, toxins, and drugs
trigger an autoimmune response
in people genetically susceptible . . ."

If she's noticed my
new diamond studs.

"Most autoimmune disorders,
unfortunately, are chronic.
But many, I'm glad to say,
can be very successfully
controlled with treatment.
In your case, most likely
inflammatory bowel disease,
also known as Crohn's disease,
your immune system appears
to be attacking healthy cells
in your terminal ileum.

"Francesca. Chess.
Am I throwing too much at you?
Do you have any questions
you'd like to ask?"

"No. Not really.
I was just wondering . . .
would you mind telling me . . .
what product
you use on your hair
to get it to curl like that?"

Forget
a little light reading
to take my mind off things.

Lotions, cute cartoons,
pretty notebook for my thoughts,
flowers to brighten up the place.

Give those to this Shannon girl,
the sick girl, with nothing
on her table but a sippy straw.

Bring me my running shoes,
a black bikini, a bottle of sriracha,
a kite, a Bernese mountain dog,

chandelier earrings that throw sparks
in the light, a ticket
to Machu Picchu.

When the nurse comes,
pleasant as I can,
I tell him no more visitors.
None. I don't want to see or
talk to anyone.

One good thing:
Looks like I lost
my phone.

Blared from sleep, I almost rip
the IV needle from my vein,
grabbing the red-flashing
bedside phone before
my clanging heart
can stop me.

"Chess!"
It's Lexie:
"I'm so upset you're sick!
Are you okay?
Are you any better?
Your mom just said—"

"We waited and waited
for you."
Bri's on, too:
"We met no one, needless to say,
and when you didn't text or call,
we figured you were still
with Berry Boy,
and when my dad came
to get us . . ."

"This is not, like, our fault,
is it?"

"No. It was fine."

Monitor Me hates
the quiver in my voice
as I picture wide-eyed,
stork-legged Lexie,

Bri, elf-small with
rowdy black hair.

"And I am so
much better.
Seriously.
No worries.
I'll be fine."

"You know, I knew
something was up with you!
I mean, cramps are supposed
to be once a month, right?
And that mono that wasn't mono
last winter? And quitting choir.
Which you love? Telling Mr. Jensen
you wouldn't try out for Ophelia,
which you could have gotten,
especially with that whole ethereal
thing you've got going lately—"

"And we finally get an invite
to Ruby's pool party and
you refuse to go?
If it wasn't for that crush
on Mr. Sugar Snap,
we wouldn't have gotten you out
of the house all summer."

"But something good
happened, right?
Something as in *Something*.
Or you'd have come back to the party.

I know this isn't the ideal time
to talk about it, but
I mean, did you guys,
you know . . ."

"Chess? It's kinda silent on your end.
Is your mom there?"

"Umm. Yes."

Lying to them,
for the first time ever,
to drive the night beetles away.

Between the curtains
I watch two ladies sit
with Shannon as she sleeps.

Hear click of knitting needles,
rustle of starched legs
crossing and uncrossing.

"See all them earrings?" the older one
tells an aide hanging
a new bag of medicine.
"She's got one for every surgery."

"Seriously?" The aide looks impressed.
Or shocked. "That's a lot of surgeries
for a young girl."

"Oh yeah. And that little cross
in the other ear? That's to keep
her from any more."

The older one counts stitches
on something pink, crinkles open
a starlight mint, sighs,

Hands another to the heavy,
younger one, whose name necklace
might say *Yvonne.*

When I wake up,
a baby hat is almost done.
The older lady stabs her needles
through the ball of yarn.

"Seems like they gave her
a double dose of sedative this time."
She hauls herself to standing,

Untangles tubes on the IV pole,
smoothes the comforter,
the pillow, the girl's jagged hair.

"Not sure how soon
we can get back, kiddo."
Yvonne leaves the mint
on Shannon's pillow,
bends to kiss her forehead,

So close to me that if she knew
I was watching through the curtain,
she could pull it aside and kiss me, too.

In a dream David sets my lips tingling
with his eyes, even in the dark.

*"I really want to kiss you.
Is it okay if . . ."*

"MWAAH!"
Stubble scrapes my cheek.
"Heyyy! How're you doing,
Chessie Chestnut?"

Strawberry-slick lips brush
my forehead.
"Hello, sweetie.
You weren't sleeping,
were you?"

"Huh?
Oh, hi, Aunt Dawn.
Hey, Uncle Charlie.
I'm doing fine."

"Because, sweetie,
I just want to tell you
the woman down the street
has what they're saying
you might have,
and as long as she stays away
from certain foods . . ."

In neon running shoes I race
through sand, sprint
through the rainbow

droplets of a sprinkler,
run straight up a waterfall,

Shoot out a purple cloud
of squid ink so no one
can see me jetting
through the ocean
on *You'll never catch me!* bubbles.

"Genetic. I looked it up online.
Cousin Joanie had it. . . .
Wouldn't surprise me a bit
if Uncle Bobby . . ."

Now if I can just stay
inside the dream.

"Dawn. Why make her upset?
Nobody's said for sure—"

Blur their voices.

"They know *something's*
very wrong. I'm no doctor
and I could tell she wasn't well
for months . . ."

But Bri's and Lexie's words
creep in like beetles:

"That time you ate
the entire bottle
of my dad's Tums . . ."

"My dad's single malt
to kill the pain . . ."

"Julia's sleepover
where you spent
the whole night
in the bathroom . . ."

"Why does everyone
in this family think
if you don't talk
about things,
if you just smile
and don't look,
or look polite
they'll, like,
miraculously . . ."

"Dawn's right, Chessie.
You had to have known
you were—"

"And I get
that you must have been hoping
it would go away—"

"Or trying to protect your mom—"

"Right. God forbid
there should be something amiss
in my sister's perfectly
constructed perfect world!"

"But protecting?
By going for a swim
in the middle
of a freezing-cold night
in the pouring rain
with some boy who
she won't even tell
anyone his name?"

"That's not the issue now.
What's important is
finding out what's—"

"Not important?
Getting home at three
in the morning?
Crying too hard to talk?"

"What happened, Chess?
I know you were sick,
but something
must have happened!"

"Did that boy push
you to do something
you weren't ready for?
Did he . . ."

"If there was a, like, asteroid
headed for the Earth?"
pipes up Natasha Oldenburg
from fifth grade,
"And the only guy you could find
was, like, Mr. Flood, the septic tank man?
Would you do it with him?"

"What about Donald Trump?
SpongeBob SquarePants?
If you knew it was your
one and only chance to ever know . . ."

"WHY DO YOU THINK
SOMETHING
'HAPPENED'?

"NOTHING HAPPENED!
AND IT WAS NOT RAINING!
AND IT DOESN'T
MATTER
ANYMORE
WHO
HE
WAS!"

My words boom
in my ears,
turn the air
Nile-bile-algae-vile

While David's words
on that endless drive home
echo in my head:

"You should have said something.
If you'd just said something . . ."

And the night beetles swarm.

The nurse sets down a basin
of warm water, soap, and paper towels
to clean up for the night.

I ask her to help me scrub
these damn wings
off my hand.

Somewhere in the clockless night,
the sobbing starts, so quiet
I have to strain to hear, so terrible
I could believe it's me,

while on my other side
Mrs. Klein demands a cab,
her pocketbook, her shoes:

"Sam, my pearls were right here
and now they're gone. Sammy,
I told you that new cleaning girl
would rob us blind. . . ."

Then, from Shannon's side again, I hear,
"Do I really need another
crazy person?
Would somebody
shut her up
before I go
friggin'
ripshit here?"

Trapped between voices,
buzzing like a fluorescent
tube about to die, I buzz
for help, wait, buzz again,
wait, until, not sure which side
of the curtain creeps me out more,

I unplug my wires from the wall,
inch my pole around
to the old lady's side, and

looking past her face,
uncurl her hand.

Her nails bite my palm;
I want to flee. But from some
forgotten corner of me
in a voice that barely quavers,
come the words I've wanted:

"It's gonna be all right.
We're here with you.
You're not alone."

Lizard eyes click open.
"Who are you?
Where's Sammy?
You stole my clothes!"

"Me? No! No. Look at me.
I don't have clothes either.
We're in the hospital.
No one here has clothes."

"Gimme that phone!"
Scraggle-haired, red-eyed,
Shannon stands beside me,
turns thumb and pinky
into a phone.
"Hello, Sam?
It's me, Shannon.

"How're you doing tonight?
So you know which shoes
she wants, right?

And you'll be here
in how long?

"No, half an hour's perfect, Sam.
Don't worry about a thing.
Mrs. Klein's doin' fine.
Just pick her out something
nice to wear, okay?
She's gonna want to look good
for going home."

Her voice gentles:
"Okay, Mrs. Klein,
he's on his way. But
traffic is terrible, he says.
So don't wait up.
He'll wake you
when he gets here.

"What's that, Sam?
Oh yeah, and he says
tell you he loves you."
Her voice wobbles as she adds,
"A bushel and a peck."

But Mrs. Klein's hand's
already eased in mine.
Her eyes flutter closed.
I stand by her bed listening
to the oxygen machine
till Shannon raises a hand
to slap me five,

and mutters
"Damn, I'm good.

"Hell, I should have
told him to bring us
a breakfast burrito
while he's at it.
And some coffee."

Her eyes slide away.
"And underpants."

I know, I know, I know.
I nod too many times.
"Bring mine, too, Sam,"
I say into my
thumb and pinky phone.

With proud, sad,
crooked smiles
we push our poles
back to our beds
to wait for sleep, or Sam.

THIRD DAY

***W**hap!*
Just as the morning cart clatter
starts, a box of tissues clips my ear.

"Case you feel like crying again."

"I won't!"
I sit up, chuck them back
the way they came.

"Missed!"

"Oh, yeah?"

I toss my tissue box over
as the vitals lady wheels in
her vitals-checking machine.

"Ha! Ya missed!"

"You girls must be feeling better,"
she says, making sure my blood's
still pumping before
I drift off again.

"**N**o reason to think . . .
every reason to believe . . .
tough disease . . . hard sometimes
to make a definitive . . .
but the tests all indicate . . .
chronic but these days . . ."

Bald-head doctor's voice
too fast, too smooth,
too jolly, hearty, way too close,
drawing squiggly pictures of intestines
as Mom nods and peppers him
with questions I can't listen to.

I don't know
this hard and tough language.
Don't speak Disease.
And I am so tired,
I close my ears until he's gone,
and through the curtain Shannon mutters:

"Duh. I could've diagnosed her
two days ago.
You don't need to be a friggin' genius
to know she's got Crohn's. Same as me.
Crohn's. Inflammatory bowel—"

"Excuse me?"

C-words ricochet
around my brain.

"You don't know me!
You know nothing about me or my . . ."

My mouth runs screaming
from the B-word.

"Mom. Could you see if this
curtain closes any tighter?"

"Fine with me.
Who said I was even talking to you?
I'm just saying, it pisses me off,
these turkeys talking about tough.
They wouldn't know tough
if it bit them on their flabby ass."

"Let's talk about happy things,"
Mom says.

"So Lily won
her tennis tournament.
Julia's loving France.
Ruby's still rafting down the Snake,
but I know she'd love
to hear from you.
In fact, everyone's
calling, texting,
worried, wondering
when they can . . .
In fact, Alexis said
if Brianna can get the car
they might be by."

"NO!
I TOLD YOU
I DIDN'T
WANT YOU TO . . .

"MOM, DID YOU TELL
THEM THAT I HAVE . . ."

A gross disease
with even grosser names.

"TELL ME
YOU DIDN'T.
BECAUSE
I DON'T, OKAY?"

Shouting to drown
the thrum of beetles.

"AND . . . IF ANYONE
ASKS YOU ANYTHING
ABOUT . . . you know . . ."

My eyes touch my hand
for wings
I know are gone.

"**C**hessie, you're acting like you
did something bad.
Like this is some kind of
terrible secret."

It's true.
Every bubble
snaking its way
down the tube
to the tub of gunk
clipped to my bed,

Each aching swallow
reminds me
of my gross
green secret,

And I wish
I could tell her, wish
we were two different people
so I could tell her.

"You're sick, sweetie.
They're your friends.
They love you.

"Here. Text them. Talk to them.
You must have dozens of texts
waiting for you.
If you had your cell."

With a plump of the pillows
and a kiss, Mom leaves me her phone.

"I'll bring the charger for you tomorrow."

"They could have mixed up
my tests with Shannon's,"
I call after her.

"Or anybody's.
It's possible, right? Doctors
make mistakes all the time.
It's possible I don't have a disease at all."

A snort hmmphs
through the curtain.

"Right. Little Miss Cupcake couldn't
have the same disease as Trailer Girl."

The Orange Croc Doc is barely
through the door before
I'm demanding a new room,
no roommate,
saying if I'm sick, it's sick
of everybody thinking
they know more
about me
than I do,

Saying loud enough
to drown out the TV's infuriating drone,
I'm the girl who always
makes the honor roll,
eats her veggies,
takes her vitamins,
runs every day.

I saved a rabbit from the neighbor's cat,
rescued a turtle from the road.
If I hadn't run to get the EpiPen when
Mom stepped on that yellow jacket nest,
she would be dead.
And not just that.
I'm a junior lifesaver,
I took CPR. . . .

So if there's any fairness
in the world, I should be fine,
not stuck here
peeing in a bedpan,
with bubbles glubbing
out my nose,

on drugs
so I can't tell
what's me, what's them,
telling me about some
alleged disease. . . .

Monitor Me hears my voice,
all whiny, huffy, pompous, prissy,
and as the Orange Croc Doc steps close,
worries the cabbage smell
I keep smelling
is in my head
or me.

Trying not to breathe
my nasty breath on her,
I tell her I am so, so sorry,
tell her these steroids
truly are evil juice,
tell her I have no time
to be sick.
Lily's winning
tennis tournaments,
Julia's biking through France,
Ruby's rafting . . .

Let her know I've already
lost the best thing
I almost had . . .

Make her see
I'd rather run
though the pain

than lose my body   my mind.

"Hang in,"
the Orange Croc Doc says,
fingers on my pulse,
worry in her eyes.

"Steroid side effects
are notoriously challenging.
Often suck, in fact.
But they're a necessary evil
to get that immune system
of yours under control."

"Like I said.
Welcome to the club."

I shiver, twitch, long
for something to barricade
my ears, my brain,

As machines beep and wheeze
and Mrs. Klein commands:
"Turn over, Sammy.
You're snoring, Sam."

And someone in another room
moans, "Nuurse! Nuuuuuurrrrse!"
and Shannon turns her TV loud, louder,

And I'm trying to hang in,
trying to be pleasant,
cooperative and pleasant,
as I tell a doc, a nurse, an aide
this isn't working for me.
I need another room.

And I know it's stupid
to think no one will call me,
see me, find me there, but
even though I haven't heard
a stir from Shannon's side
in hours,

I tell them, "Get me out of here!"

"**P**oor you!"
"Look at you!
"I can't believe . . ."
"Don't sit up, Chess. It's fine!"

All glowy tan in shorts and tanks,
ponytails still wet from pool or gym,
Lexie and Bri burst into my stale
green-curtained den, and before
I can warn them I've had nothing
but a sponge bath since,
well . . . you know . . . that night,
I'm wrapped up in their arms.

"We couldn't decide
whether to bring like, reading matter,
or go with . . ."
Bri ties a blue *GET WELL* balloon
to my IV pole, dumps
from her shopping bag
a box of pink Peeps bunnies,
rhinestone flip-flops,
a puzzle book,
a whiskery stuffed mouse.

"It's amazing what you can find
at the ninety-nine-cent store.
Care for a four-month-old Peep?
Your mom said you can't have
any food, but everyone knows
Peeps don't qualify."

"How're you feeling today?
Your mom said you gave her
a really bad—"

"Not that you look that sick. No.
Seriously. I mean your face
is a little poufy. And your eyes
look a little weird—"

Both carefully not staring
at med bags, bedpan, tubes.

"So. Now that your mom's not here.
Does Chessie have a boyfriend?"
asks Bri, determinedly perky.
"You still haven't said
if you heard from him."

"Or told us where he lives.
Or where he goes to school.
Or if he's, like, a farmer person."

"Never mind that.
Has he texted? Called?"

Night beetles chitter
in my ears.
"No.
And even if he wanted to . . ."

My eyes won't meet their eyes.
My mouth won't shape his name.
". . . my phone's lying
on the bottom of the lake."

"What? What happened?
What's that mean?"

I can feel beetle feet
creeping
closer.

"Does he know
how sick you are?"

"Should we go out to Sugar Snap
Farm and, like, reconnoiter?"

"No!
Please.
No!"

Sticky feelers
flick my eyelids.

"Oh. By the way. I hate
to bring this up now, but
Jake is having a party next week,
and hope, for some reason,
springs eternal, so, not that I think
you'll still be sick then,
but if you could tell your mom
I'm gonna need my dress back . . ."

And I wonder what
would happen
if I didn't say,
"No worries,"

Didn't assure
them yes, of course,

by then
I'll definitely
be fine,

Tried saying,
Listen.
Something
really bad
happened with David.

I can give you the money
for the dress. But
if I tell you,
will you promise
not to tell?

But Monitor Me,
floating alongside
the blue balloon, sees
the scared in their smiles,

Like the smiles we smiled
at Patrick Morrissey's sister
when she came to third grade
with her prosthetic arm,
like we smiled at the dead-eyed ladies
slumped in their wheelchairs,
the year we sang holiday songs
at the nursing home.

"Excuse me, ladies."
The nurse smiles, too,
as she sweeps the bedpan

off the chest of drawers,
announces, "Good news, Francesca!
We're giving you an upgrade!"
Returns with what looks like
an old lady's walker with a toilet seat
between its legs.
"Ta-da! Your new commode!
Enjoy!"

And they smile
till they leave
in a whoosh
of kisses, wishes,
and relief
that they're
not me and
they are
outta here.

And in the silence
left by all the words
unsaid,
it's pretty clear

I've stepped
off the edge
of my life

Into Sickland.

No! I crank my bed up,
slide feet into my new flip-flops,
unplug, unsnarl, unhook
my nose-tube tub,
rehook the tubes to my IV pole,
wrestle its wheels around
the heinous commode.

No! There are no night beetles
in the daylight,

Just spots dancing
in the corners
of my eyes.

And I'm walking,
right?

Walking.

Tile by tile,
step after step,
past the doctors
leaving Shannon's bed.

Hang in, the Orange Croc Doc said.
That chitter in my ears
is just the hum
of the machines.
Or evil juice.

The face waiting
in the bathroom mirror
will not be me.

Only six
more tiles to go.

And who said
I have to look?
Just pee.

Stand clear of the mirror,
brush tongue, teeth, scrub armpits
with someone's Listerine,
rake hair into a lump,
no pencil like the Orange Croc Doc's
to hold it up, stab someone's toothbrush through,
twist tendrils till they agree to curl,
pinch cheeks, bite color to my lips.

"I like the little peach-fuzzy hairs
on your lip," he said.
"You're telling me I have
a mustache."
"No. They're nice. I like
the way they feel."

Now if I just climb up on the toilet,
I can see if my belly looks
as giant as it feels,
if the rest of me looks fat.

Please, God, not that!

If it weren't for all these
stupid tubes tangling,
and this damn balloon!

Oh, no!

Forget the pinpoint eyes, hair like roadkill,
skin like someone who's been floating
facedown in a river for a month or two.

There's nothing
in my nose.

Above me the blue balloon bobs.
Somewhere down my chest,
the tube with three greenish bubbles
caught in its coils.

"I don't know what happened,"
I tell the nurse who rushes
to the bathroom
when I ring.

She glares like I'm a dog
who piddled on her floor.

"What do you mean,
what happened?
You pulled
it out.
Your doctor
is not
going to be
pleased."

"No. It must have fallen out!
I WOULD NEVER . . . I SWEAR!
I'M NOT THE KIND OF PERSON WHO . . ."

And yet,
do I know?

"**H**ow 'bout we give it a try
without the tube,"
the Orange Croc Doc says.
"We'll put the tube back
if we need to. . . ."

"No! Please! No!"

She's talking blood counts,
this rate, that rate, numbers
I can't understand.

"Meanwhile, why don't I ask
for someone
to come down from psych
so we can get you a bit
more comfortable,"
she says, so brisk and tender
with her corkscrew curls,

All I can do is nod
and try to smile.

Tassel loafers,
clipboard, blue blazer,
laser-blue eyes:
"So I hear you're having a rough time.
What's up?"

He looks more college admissions officer
than shrink.

I pull out my interview smile.
"Not much. Besides me, that is.
Sitting up.
In this chair, I mean.
Plus, I just took my first walk.
To the bathroom.
And my doctor says
I'm doing fine."

"That's good news. Now why don't
you tell me what's been going on.
Then we'll see what we can do
to make you more comfortable."

"Another pill?
Because, my theory?
I'm not that sick anymore.
It's just, no one has any clue
how I am, because of the drugs
they've got me on."

"That's an interesting theory, Francesca.
And we can talk about it.
But first we just need to get through
a few routine questions.

"Would you mind telling me
what year it is?"

Would you mind telling me
why you're looking at me
the way they look at Shannon?
Not just like I might be
a crazy person,

But like I'm one of those tiny
transparent guppies
Mom bought for me
that swam in circles
for a day, then, belly-up, floated to . . .

abscess

　　remission　flare-up

　　　　immuno-something

　　treatment goals

Doctor words
I thought I hadn't heard
flash like fireworks
in my brain.

"Francesca, can you tell me
who's the president of
the United States?"

. . . *activation of immune system*

leads to influx

of inflammatory cells

to the intestine . . .

. . . once activated,

the immune system doesn't shut off,

resulting in chronic

inflammation . . .

. . . disturbs immune system's ability

to distinguish between self

and nonself . . .

"Francesca, would you be
more comfortable
lying down?"

"NO! I mean, no, thank you."

And I keep hanging on
by my politeness,
giving him the answers
he's looking for, until

Monitor Me hears my tiny transparent
guppy voice ask: "If I do

have whatever this is,
am I going to die?"

The shrink sets down his clipboard.
Leans in closer.

I watch his eyebrows knit,
his Adam's apple bob,
his lips tighten for an instant
before he speaks
of perfectly understandable concern,
normal to worry, not saying
there won't be challenges, but . . .

I wait for *Die? You?*
Of course not!
Don't be ridiculous!

Wait through cautious, useless
doctor words.
Wait for him to go.

"**D**octor! Wait!
Come back!

"Like, for example, that girl
in the bed next to me?
Her body is basically out to get her?
Hates *her* as much as she hates *it*?
That's what 'autoimmune' means?

"And 'chronic' means
no matter how good
she thinks she feels,
it's got her?
She's got it?
She's.
It?

"Is that
what everyone is saying?"

"Francesca," he says. "I can't speak
to what others might have said,
but I can assure you, no matter what
disease you may or may not have,
you'll still be you."

"But what's that mean?"

I've been trying to whisper
in case Shannon's listening
through the curtain, but
his careful kindness
cracks my voice
wide open:

"Who's 'you' when
your own body is
your biggest enemy?

"If her own body
can't recognize
her, how can she?"

"You're asking important questions.
It might take a while
to figure out the answers.
But right now, I think
what we need to do
is give you something to calm
your nerves and let you sleep."

"No! Doctor. You don't understand!
If I lie down and sleep,
if I die, I'll never know!"

"YO! NO DYING HERE!
GOT THAT?"

Shannon's voice slices
through the curtain.

"NOBODY DIES IN MY ROOM!
INCLUDING ME!"

"Leap, ladies! Leap over the lake!
Don't let those feet get wet!
Tummies in! Arms out!
Heads up!"

I soar above the mirror-shiny floor,
land easy as a dragonfly. "Perfect!"
Ms. Filipova bestows her chilly smile,
whispers to my mom:

"Remember what a clumsy little girl
she was? No turnout, no elevation,
those pudgy legs. She dances
so much better dead."

To the easy music of the waves
I dance with David in the dark.
Bonfire sparks glint in his eyes.
He swoops me into the air. I fly,

Swim beside him in the lake.
Damselflies skim over us.
Words waft in
from miles away.

It is so pleasant being dead, so easy
floating naked here with David
in the ocean,
waveless now, and warm.

Words drift in . . .

"Couldn't you just sneak her up
in the middle of the night?

"She'd be so good, Mom.
I know she would.
She wouldn't make a sound."

Drift out . . .

"Oh, baby, you know
we can't do that."

"But I miss her so much."

"That's why we need to
get you better.
So you can be with her again."

"Couldn't you just bring her
underneath the window
so I could wave?"

In fading light I wake
to a headache and a tray:
cold tea, melted orange icey,
yellow Jell-O.

A doctor voice wishes Shannon
good night.

In the hall a cigarette-voiced man yells,
"You guys with your million-dollar
machines and thousand-dollar pills!"

Mrs. Klein, on her imagined phone,
orders a salmon steak,
enough for two,
make sure it's fresh this time.

I hear Shannon crying.

And with the dark
the night beetles gather.
I hear their oil-slick shells rattle,
feel the prickle of their legs,
the tickle of their feelers.

"DON'T TELL ME
VISITING HOURS ARE OVER
AND DON'T TELL ME TO CALM DOWN!"
yells the hall man.

"I'LL CALM DOWN
WHEN SOMEBODY STOPS SPOUTING
MEDICAL MUMBO JUMBO AND STARTS
MAKING HER BETTER!"

Their vinegar stink stings
my nostrils,
their whisper weight masses,
making ready, marching
to my heart's drumming.

"I'LL CALM DOWN
WHEN YOU STOP
TALKING ABOUT
CUTTING HER OPEN.

"I'LL CALM DOWN WHEN YOU
JUST TELL ME. WHEN. ARE.
YOU. GONNA. MAKE. HER
BETTER?"

When I was little,
waiting for the night to end,

my dad could always
scare away the night beetles.

I have no legs, no voice,
can only clench myself closed, try
to fly my mind somewhere safe
as the night beetles swarm.

And I whisper to the dark:

"I wish I could be just me.
Without my body."

Then through the curtain,
so soft
I hardly know
it's her:

"Sometimes it helps
if you imagine purring.
One of those big old stripey—
I'll just stand here on your pillow
and keep this going all night
long as you don't do something
to annoy me—
tomcats with a rumbling purr
that quiets down your breath
and helps your heart un-hurt.

"Anyway. That's what works
for me sometimes."

"I had a cat when I was little.
Bobo. My dad used to tuck her in
with me at night.

"That Cupcake thing?
That's what he called me back then.
And I'm not saying
it was my goal in life:
'So, Chess, what do you want to be
when you grow up?'
'Oh, I want to be a fattening pastry item.'

"And I realize
the cupcake bottom line
is, you get eaten,
but I felt so . . .

"I mean . . . who doesn't
love a cupcake?
Small and perfect.
Neat. Sweet . . .

"If it were up to me
I wouldn't even
have
bowels,

"Never mind
a disease
with 'bowel'
its middle name.

"'Oh, hello! I'm Chess!
I have a bowel disease!
I'm gonna be spending my life
looking for a bathroom!'

"Not happening.
I do not
have it.
I refuse.

"At least cancer,
even the meanest person
wouldn't be all *'Ewwwwww!'*
behind your back,
or, when they see you,
trying not to look away.

"I mean, sick
is the last thing
you're supposed
to be thinking about
on an island in the middle
of a lake in the middle
of the night with a boy
like no boy you've met before.

"He was the first boy
I liked who ever really . . .
you know . . .
wanted me.

"Shannon?
Y'awake over there?"

"Yeah. But this pity-party shit
is getting on my nerves.

"They can't take shit,
who needs 'em."

"Could you stop saying
that word, please?"

"Oh, does Cupcake like
the D-word better?
Cuz you know, diarrhea
can be your friend."

"I said, stop!"

"Excuse me, Mr. Teacherperson.
This exam takes how long?
Because I think you should know
I have this little diarrhea problem—"

"I DON'T WANT TO HEAR
THIS!"

"Oh, Aunt Mabel,
I'd love to clean your garage.
But unless you got a bathroom close by,
and I mean REALLY close . . ."

"SHANNON!"

"And you don't even have to say
the D-word, but trust me, if you do,
no one will mess with you.
They don't need to know
your pills got it under control."

"Pills?
There are pills?
Besides the evil juice?"

"Oh yeah.
They got all kinds of pills.
Pills, shots, shit they drip into you . . ."

"That work?
Because
I mean, if
they work,
how come
you're so sick?

"Sorry!
I shouldn't
have said that!
I'm so sorry!"

"And it's not like psoriasis
or something where the whole world
can see what you have.
You might feel like crap, but
to people who don't know
you have a disease,
you look fine.

"Except for if you get the acne
and the fat face
from the evil juice,
or your hair gets thin and weird.
Like mine.

"But you know what?
Most people are too busy
worrying how *they* look
to be thinking about you.

"Unless the evil juice
makes you blow up
like a balloon.

"Which obviously never
happened to me. In fact,
I could stand to gain—"

"If I get fat again
I'll die!"

"Would you shut up about dying?
I've been in and outta here
since I was ten, okay?
And do I look dead to you?
Don't answer that!

"Forget dying.
Forget fat.
Forget necessary evil.
There's only one necessary thing
and that's to get it through your head:

"We don't take stress.
We give stress.

"Which is why
you need to lose this 'sorry' shit.

Someone comes to take your blood,
and you're like: 'Oh, thank you!
How much would you like?
Oh, have some more!'

"Uh-uh! 'Go away! I barely
got enough to keep me going here!'
Why d'you need to be all meek
and shit?

"You're the one sick!
And you're worrying
some boy
won't like
you for it?

"Does that
sound right to you?

"Yo. Are you even listening?
You didn't go to sleep on me, did you?"

"I can't be sick.
I've got this really busy life:
this summer job, plus
going to look at colleges.
Plus, I'm planning
to go out for track, so
I've been doing a lot of running.

"When I wasn't feeling too bad.

"Cuz I haven't been feeling
all that good these last months.

"Plus, we had this whole plan—
those friends who were here before,
and me—to be, like, bolder, social-wise,
more out there. Not that we'd ever
be as cool as this girl Julia and her . . ."

"Shannon, you still awake?
I thought you'd make a crack
or something."

"Nah. Just thinking."

"So I'm walking to school
scuffing my hand along
one of those dusty hedges,
feeling pretty good,
with my little uniform skirt
rolled up all short, and the lip gloss
my mom thought she hid
making my lips all juicy,
and here's this dandelion
sticking its nose
out of the top of a bush,
four feet in the air.

"And it's not even a daisy,
but I nip its head off cuz I just know
God put it there so I can find out if
Anthony Morabito in my homeroom
loves me or loves me not.

"And it's got like a jillion teensy
petals, but this is important, right?
So I pinch them, one by one,
till there's nothing but a pile of yellow.

"And yeah, he loved me,
for about ten minutes,
and what made me think of this now
I don't know.
But I keep on thinking

"If that dandelion made it through
those sticks and branches,
taller than any dandelion is supposed

to grow, taller than Anthony,
most likely,
tall as it needed to be
to reach the light,
it had to have made another flower.
That can't have been the only one, right?"

"If we could order
any ice cream flavor
in the world? Right now?
What kind would you get?"

"That's easy. A root beer float.
Three scoops of vanilla, maybe four,
mountain of real whipped cream,
not the squirty shit—"

"I'd get that way-too-green pistachio
with the cherries,
the kind they only have—"

"Yeah, yeah.
In old-timey Chinese restaurants.
I used to love—"

"Me too.

"I could call my mom
to bring us some.

"If morning ever—"

From the hall, I hear:

"I KNOW WHAT TIME IT IS!
I'M FAMILY.
I CAN VISIT
ANY DAMN TIME

I WANT!
YOU KNOW WHERE I DROVE FROM?
HOW FAR I CAME
TO SEE MY LITTLE GIRL
BEFORE YOU PEOPLE . . ."

"Oh, no! It's that man again!"

"Sir. I'm going
to have to—"

"I LOVE YOU,
HONEY!

"EXCUSE ME.
DO NOT
TOUCH ME.
TAKE YOUR HANDS
OFF ME. I'M
HER FATHER.

"YOU CAN'T
TELL ME TO LEAVE."

"Yes, sir. I can.
You can come back
in the morning."

"NO.
YOU
CAN'T!"

"Shannon?"

"Is that
your dad?"

Picturing a dad wiry, scraggly
like her.
Bulky tall, like mine.

Picturing flinching, bracing,
flinging, sinking
into the arms
of someone you're never sure
you want to see.

"NO. JUST
SOME DRUNK
ASSHOLE
NO ONE
WANTS HERE."

"You don't have to tell me
about not wanting anyone
to see you like this.

"Or about dads . . .

"I mean, it was a long time ago,
that Cupcake thing.

"So long I hardly think about him
Except, you know, times like this."

"**O**ne ear was bigger than the other
and stuck out and, when he rode
me on his shoulders,
made the perfect turn signal
and an even better handle when I hooked

"My other arm around to honk his nose.
He'd bugle like a bike horn,
Ooga-ooga like a clown.
Then, all outraged
innocence, go, 'What's funny?'

"Or, 'What, do I look like a horse to you?'
when I yanked his ear
and hollered 'Giddyap!'
'Yes!' I'd go, and
he'd bray and sputter.

"I actually scrutinized my left ear
every time I passed a mirror,
eager for the Ear of Distinction,
as he called it,
doing his Mount Rushmore face,
then wiggling both his ears until I smiled.

"I'm over it. Obviously. Who wants an ear
that sticks out through your hair?
Plus, this has to be your basic
corny dad story.
No doubt every daddy in the universe
does the old honking horsey ride.

"No doubt he's cracking up

the new kid now.
Unless the new wife
made him pin the ear back.
Or the new kid bit it off."

"I'll shut up now.
I know I'm blabbing.

"And I know I'm supposed to stop
being sorry, but I'm so sorry
I said that to the shrink
about your body hating you,
being out to get you.

"About you having something . . .
you know . . . chronic."

"Yeah, well . . .

"The good news is
chronic ain't fatal.

"Except when
you die from it."

"Yeah, but what kind of life
do you have? If you even
have a life.

"And what exactly
does 'inflammation' mean?"

Picturing flames licking
through her guts,
barbeque briquettes
smoldering holes
in her insides.

"Shannon. That island
I was talking about before?
That night?"

And my insides
burn, my blood
throbs and bubbles,
and I can't tell if
it's a surge of evil juice,
or a temp of 108,
or where my mind
keeps taking me.

"Shannon? Something
really bad happened.

"With that boy.

"I was thinking
about telling—
I mean, they've been
my best friends
since preschool—

"But it was Lexie's brand-new dress
I was wearing that night.

"And not just that.
It was like . . . it felt like
we're from different planets.
Like they're in Cupcake World.
And I'm on, I don't know, Uranus."

And I want her to laugh,
make a sixth-grade joke,
say, Well I hope you're
not planning on telling *me*,
because I've got all the shit
I can handle.
Say something.

"And now it's like someone's peeling
my skin off with a potato peeler.
Like I'm feeling the feelings
of every sick person
in this hospital,
and I can't make it go away.

"It seems easier
to just die."

        "Don't say that! Don't ever
        say that!"

"I wish I could stay
a cupcake.

"I wish your cat was here."

        "What cat?"

"The cat you were talking about
purring on your chest all night."

        "I don't have a cat."

"But I heard you asking
your mom to smuggle—"

"HEY! DID I ASK YOU TO EAVESDROP
ON MY PRIVATE CONVERSATIONS?"

"No, but I mean, here we are—"

"RIGHT! TWO SORRY-ASS SICK GIRLS
STARING AT THE CEILING!
THAT DOESN'T MEAN YOU
CAN . . . I'VE GOT NO TIME
FOR THIS!
I'VE GOT THINGS TO DO!"

"Stop yelling!
I'm trying to tell you something.

"Those things
I said?

"About you
being sick?

"It was cuz I'm lying here
trying to get my mind around . . .

"Shannon.
What if

"it's not
just *your*

body that's . . . ?

"And please
don't be like
Duhhh!
because—"

"Yeah. That was my dad, okay?

"And I have a daughter.
Not a cat.

"A baby girl."

You?
Baby?
With Anthony Morabito?
So that was, like, a parable?
Are you still with him?
Or with someone else?
Where is she?
Aren't you too sick
to take care of her?
What's gonna . . .

But I would no more ask her
than . . .

"Her name is Joya.
She's with my other grandmother
in Atlantic City.
Might as well be Uranus.

"And if you ask me one question

or say 'sorry,' I'm gonna have to
come over there and kick your sorry
sick-girl ass."

"**C**hess. Y'asleep?"

"No. Just lying here.
Thinking about that night."

I almost
tell her then.
How it started out so beautiful,
so magically, amazingly beautiful . . .

"This disease ought to come with amnesia.
You know that?

"Shannon? You sleeping?"

"If I was sleeping would I be asking
if you're sleeping?

"You feeling any better?"

"No.
That stuff the shrink gave me?
That's supposed to be making me sedate
and tranquil?
It's not working.
I'm gonna call the nurse
to give me more."

"**S**he's so quiet tonight,
Mrs. Klein."

"Yeah. Where's old Sam
when we need him?"

"Chess?
I was thinking about opening
the curtain.

"Is that
okay with you?"

"Open'd be good."

"We could use some air."

"Listen. If I die
will you send me flowers?
And don't tell me I'm not dying.
I know that. But
if I do?"

"I'll totally send you flowers."

"Then I'll send you some, too.
But I don't want ugly cheap-ass ones.
Carnations and shit.
Or gladiolas.
I hate gladiolas.

"There was an old lady
at my church named Gladiola.
She was ugly, too."

"Don't worry.
I even hate the word 'gladiola.'"

"Get me red roses.
So many my eyes will bug out
even though I'm dead. So many
I can smell them through my coffin.

"What should I get you?"

"Red roses will do."

"Or we could send each other
something now.
Without dying.

Because, I mean,
if we both die,
we're basically fucked."

In a shoe just big enough
for her body, a girl bobs
on the ocean.

A tiny girl
bob-bobbing
in a wooden shoe

Too high
to see over,
too tight to turn

Her head can't lift
her arms to row.
No wind to blow

The shoe to shore,
no one to hear
her scream.

"**S**hannon?
Do you believe in dreams?

"Shannon?
You didn't go to sleep on me,
did you?"

And I know
dreams are just dreams,

Know Shannon is just sleeping,
and the four docs in shower caps

Swooshing closed the curtains
around her bed will make her better;

Know the pill the nurse
gives me will let me sleep at last.

The bells, beeps, buzzes, urgent
voices I hear can only be a dream.

Surely I imagine the rubber squeak
of a bed pushed out the door, and later

In this endless night imagine
Mrs. Klein's bed, too,

Wheeled out past mine:

Hallucinate her
sepulchral croak:

"Dead as a mackerel
on a tray."

In the hall carts clank.
Nurse voices discuss the weather.
Night beetles shriek and chitter.

I want to cry out for my mom, my dad,
another pill to kill the dreaming,
let me burrow deep and deeper.

But I can't
stop thinking

You can simply
stop being

In the dark
with nobody to see.

FOURTH DAY

"Hey there, Champ!"

"Shh! Steve! Let her sleep.
We haven't seen that sweet smile
since she stayed with us
the summer things went bad,
and she'd wake up
crying for her daddy,
and you'd sing
'Bridge Over Troubled Water'
and she'd climb into your lap
and you'd promise her
we'd never let anything else . . ."

"No, it was that other song
by what's-his-name . . ."

"Right, right.
The one who's bald now."

"We're all bald now.
It's Poppy, Cupcake.
Poppy and Nana."

"To get you all cleaned up
and pretty."

It is so pleasant being dead,
so easy, lulled by the rain
streaming the windows,
pummeling the roof,

In neutral, slowly rolling
in rhythm with the flapping,

flopping, foaming, slapping.
Smoothing, stroking,
stroking, soothing,

"New nail polish . . . sushi pajamas . . .
so adorable . . . tuna, eel and cucumber,
California roll, wasabi green . . .

"Don't you feel better all clean
and spiffy with your pretty pink toes?

"That nice doctor says
You're doing better
and better.

"See all the cards you got
And those gorgeous pink roses?"

"Shannon sent me roses?"

"Barb, did she just say something?"

"I don't think so.
So nice to finally have a little peace
and quiet in here. So nice to have
the room to ourselves!"

"Excuse me, Nurse,
we'd like to get her out of this gown
and into these new pajamas.
Would you give us a hand?"

It is so easy being me, three,
clean and coddled, cuddled

hearing, not hearing,
hearing, not caring,

Here outside of time
inside the car-wash storm.

"**S**hould we say something to her, Steve?
About . . . you know . . ."

"The birthday party?
It's your birthday, Cupcake.
Did you remember today's—"

"No, Steve. The . . . other thing.
Both other things."

"Barb, no need to upset her
till she's feeling better."

Icicles of light
prickle,
swirl,
shatter.

Monitor Me tastes
my stagnant mouth,
hears my voice,
creaky as Mrs. Klein's:
"What other things?"

"Well, good morning,
Sleeping Beauty!"

Sees me fumble
through rumpled bedding
for the button
to raise my aching head.

"WHAT TIME IS IT?
WHAT HAPPENED?"

There has to be some clicker,
button, windshield wiper
to unfog this . . .

"Sweetie, I'm afraid there were some . . .
developments in the—"

"Barb!
It's okay, Chessie.
This is no time to think
about anything but getting better.
Everything. Is. Fine."

"Look. They left your breakfast tray.
Would you like a little . . ."

"Developments?
With SHANNON?"

Yo! No dying here!
Nobody dies in my room.
Including me!

"WHERE IS SHE?
WHERE'S SHANNON?"

"You didn't even like her, sweetie."

"Barbara!"

"It's true. The nurse told us
you practically demanded
a different room."

"Chessie!
What are you doing?
Please!
You're in no shape to . . .
CAREFUL OF THOSE TUBES!"

I fight to keep the walls
from wobbling,
floor from cracking
into a kaleidoscope,

Ignore the roaring
in my ears, my head
giraffe-far
from my feet,
legs limp
as rubber bands.

"Chessie, watch out
for the pole!"

"Steve, help her
with that curtain!"

In the bed by the window,
a stranger snores.

And where Shannon's bed was,
air.

No fallen card
or crumpled straw

To show that either one
was there.

"NOOOOOOO!

"SHE SAID NO DYING HERE!"

Foot catches.

Water splashes.

Vase shatters.

Roses scatter.

I stumble
to the floor.

"Nurse!
Steve! Get the nurse!"

"She tripped, that's all.
She's fine.
Chess. You're okay, right?"

"NO! SHE PROMISED ME NO DYING!"

"**S**hhh."
Soft nurse hands
lift me into bed,
pull the curtains.

"Shhh.
She was very, very sick
for a very long time.
And last night, I'm sorry to say,
she expired."

"Expired?
You mean
SHE'S DEAD?"

"Yes. Poor Mrs. Klein.
She's in a better place."

"NO! MY FRIEND SHANNON,
WHO I PROMISED
ROSES."

"I know, cookie. I know.
That was a tough night,
last night. First Mrs. K.,
then that little girl
rushed off to surgery.
But don't worry.
You're doing fine.
You're gonna be—"

"She's not dead?"

"That scrappy little girl?
Uh-uh. Her surgery took longer
than—"

"She didn't say anything
about . . . HOW COULD SHE NOT
TELL ME?"

"Shhh.
It was an emergency,
She didn't know.
But don't worry. She'll be back.
That little girl's a fighter.
Just like you."

I cry for Mrs. Klein.

I sleep.

Eat half
a scrambled egg,

Let doctors measure,
push, and poke,

Listen to them praise
my progress,
urge me to sit up,
try a walk.

I open my curtain,
walk to the visitor chair
beside the space
where Shannon's
bed should be, sit,

And wait.
Listen to the new lady
in Mrs. Klein's bed
grumble on the phone
behind her curtain
and scold the nurse.

Wait.
Try not to watch the clock.
Or let my mind jump to David
before I read the florist card
that came with the pink roses:
Eleanor and Jared Kaye.

Read the sushi names
on my ridiculous pajamas.
Push zucchini, rice, and
some nameless fish fillet
around my plate.

Try not to think
of Lake George summers
whacking heads off trout,
slicing their bellies open,
pulling out shiny blue-pink guts,
scraping clean their flesh.

Try not to picture
Shannon's scalpeled belly,
Shannon's guts tossed
in a bucket.

Think about a haircut,
pepperoni pizza,
if Mom's picked up my paycheck,
new size 2 skinny jeans,
possibly tangerine,

Till muscles twitch, nerves itch,
and if there's no proof soon
Shannon is okay,
I'm going to explode.

Teetery baby   step
Doddering old lady   step

Past the bathroom
through the door

Hopscotch square
by square

Into the fluorescent
hall hubbub

In my rhinestone flip-flops
and embarrassing pajamas.

Step   step
past gurneys, carts, computers,

Past an old man parked
in a wheelchair who calls, "You go, girl!"

Step.   One hand on the pole
the other on the wall

Legs noodling
but still moving

Step.   Okay.
I can see

The nurses' station.
The Orange Croc Doc on her phone.

"You okay, my love?"
asks a nurse.

I catch my breath
and say I'm fine.

I really do mean
to ask the Orange Croc Doc
about Shannon. But:

"Doctor? Is my . . . you know . . .
what you said I might . . ."

"Your Crohn's disease?"

My eyes won't look at her.
Head can't get itself to nod.

"That's what I have?
For sure? Crohn's?"

And I don't know if my knees tremble
from the evil-sounding word,
the walk, or evil juice,

If the hot hollow
in my belly is hunger
or inflammation eating my insides,

If this spinny weakness means
I'm sicker, or just starting to feel
the sickness that's been
inside me all along.

"Guess I'm just lucky
I don't need an operation, right?
Like Shannon?"

Down the hall, a man
with a limp stops pacing,
hurries toward us.

"I don't. Right, Doc?"

"Not now, no. And hopefully,
we can continue to manage your
disease medically."

"Hopefully?
Does that mean you don't know?"

"Doc!"
Cigarette voice,
spattered work boots,
Shannon's dragon eyes:

"They took her in at six!
It's half past one!
What's goin' on?"

"Just a minute, Mr. Williams.
Chess, Crohn's is an
unpredictable disease.
I can't promise you won't—"

"Yeah, and even if she did,
we know what her
promises are worth!"

His cane jabs the air.
"You people promised
no more surgery.
Said there'd be nothing left
if you kept cutting,
and now . . .
I told her mom

she should have taken her
down to New York.
Or Boston.
Anywhere
but here!"

The Orange Croc Doc touches my arm.
"We'll talk more later, Chess.
Walk with me, Mr. Williams."

Beetles rattle in my ears,
cloud my eyes as she leads
him toward the elevator,

And I want to follow,
find out what they're saying,

Or scream: No!
Come back!
Talk to me now!

But Monitor Me hears my voice
hollow-bright as Nana's:

"She'll be okay.
Don't worry, Mr. Willliams.
Shannon will be fine."

"**H**appy birthday, darling!"

"I told you we'd
bring the party to you!"

"Here's our beautiful girl!"

"Hey. Chess."

Mom, Nana, Poppy,
Charlie, Dawn, and
Cousin Kimmy
hug me, kiss me.

"Have some sparkling cider.
A cupcake.
Your doctor said it's fine.
They're so good.
I bought a ton
in case friends come."

"Mother." Dawn and Mom
exchange raised-eyebrow glances.
"Where on earth
did you find those pajamas?"

Poppy launches into
"Happy Birthday."

"Excuse me!"
The lady in Mrs. Klein's bed
clears her throat.

"I happen
to be a very
sick woman."

"We're sorry, sweetie,
it's just—"

"My name,
for your information,
is not Sweetie.
I taught Language Arts
in the Albany schools
for forty-one years.
My name is Mrs. Murch."

Kimmy chokes
back giggles,

Nana offers
Mrs. Murch a cupcake,

Poppy pulls in chairs,
pulls out jokes,

While Mom wonders if she dares
have a cupcake, since it is my birthday,

And Aunt Dawn wonders if we wouldn't
be more comfortable in the lounge,

And Mrs. Murch mutters she'd
be more comfortable, that's for sure,

And I try to find smiles,
thanks, not now thanks,

When all I want is to jump free
of this body and disappear.

And finally,
Green Jacket Man ferrying the bed,

A nurse unhooking,
hooking, docking,

Her mom and grandma,
hovering,

And Shannon,
tiny, tubed,

Lifting a limp hand to wave,
and in a voice scratchy

From the tube down her nose,
mumbling to Mrs. Murch,

"Has anyone ever told you
you look like a bullfrog?"

Before her eyes
drift away,

Her curtain
closed.

"Grrrmph!"
goes Mrs. Murch,
so froggily
I have to turn my hoot
into a cough

As moms and grandmas,
trying for smoothing smiles,
hurry to explain
it must be the anesthesia,
the morphine, the steroids
making people say things
they'd never say
and certainly don't mean,

That Mrs. Murch
bears no resemblance
whatsoever to a frog
of any sort!

"I happen
to be a very sick woman,"
garrumphs Mrs. Murch,
and I laugh, laugh,
can't stop
laughing.

"She's never like this,"
Mom assures them, and
I laugh
until I'm crying,
crying,
crumpled,
crying.

"This isn't her.
She'll be herself again
soon as she's had some sleep.
Don't worry. She'll be fine."

"Right! Like Shannon's fine!
Like Mrs. Klein is fine!"

Rage hotter than lava,
eviler than evil juice
roars in my ears,
floods my belly,
blurs my eyes.

"Because I'm
the Queen of Fine.
Or is that you, Mom?
You tell me I'm fine.
I tell you I'm fine.
That's the deal, right?
Ever since Dad.
Keep it quiet.
Keep it nice.
Everyone is fine."

Monitor Me
feels me
sliding, skidding,
fishtailing
on black ice

As they pat me, hug me,
"it's okay" me, assure me
I'm so much better,
things always feel worse
before they get better.

Monitor Me tries
to pull me back,

talk me down,
remind me
they're just scared.

I tell Monitor Me
to fuck off, tell Bri's
obnoxious blue balloon
with its cheery *GET WELL*
to fuck off, too.

And fuck this tremble in my voice:
"There *is* no *better* here.
This is me.
With a horrible disease
that never goes away.

"Can you protect me
from that?
Can anyone
protect anyone
from anything?

"Because
I am sick
to death
of protecting
you!"

I rip the balloon string
from my IV pole.
Stomp it,
stomp it
till it pops.

"What was that?"
cries Mrs. Murch.

"Me, telling everyone
to GO AWAY!"

Part of me wants
to rewind time,
hug ugly words away,

Grab their hands
as Shannon's mom throws mine
a look like: Welcome to the club!

Beg them, as they fumble
for bags and pocketbooks, please
don't leave me here alone.

But the rage flows,
shocking and unstoppable
as shit.

I turn my back on them.
Climb into bed.

"Come on, now.
I don't want to hear
that kind of talk."
The nurse taps a pill
from a tiny pleated cup
into my hand.

"You don't hate yourself.
After the day you had,
who wouldn't be a little stressed?
And you and I both know
you don't hate them.

"Have a little more water, cookie.
Take some good deep breaths.
I'm gonna lower your bed for you
and you're gonna take your mind
someplace calm and peaceful.
Someplace beautiful.
That's a good girl."

Her voice warmed
from a scold to a caress.

And there I am,
back on the island
in Lexie's gauzy, flowery,
brand-new dress,
which we're already calling
her good-luck dress because
it's so much cooler
than the stuff we wear,
and it's not nearly warm enough,
not even with my jean jacket,
but it's so beautiful,

Giant moon, bazillion stars,
canoe floated off somewhere
among the water lilies,
marooned,
like something in a movie
or a song,

And he's kissing,
touching
like no boy
has touched me,
and even through the pain,
"no" melts into "maybe,"
"maybe" begins to . . .

But then
this churning
roiling burning

fainting feeling
starts and

I can't
do anything
to stop it.

And first
I'm just afraid
I'll puke,
but then

There's the
smell.

And I try to jump
into the lake
before it's too late,

But
it's   too   late.

And I try to swim away
from the stink,
from the mess,
from poor David,
who, baffled,
or maybe horrified,
has jumped in after me,

And the water's so cold
I'm sure I'll die,
but it's numbing
the pain enough
so I can keep
swimming,

trying to kick
my underpants off
and swim at the same time,
praying the water
will wash off the mess
before he catches me,
terrified I've ruined
Lexie's dress,

And it's starting to rain,
and the whole swim
back to shore,
the whole wet, wordless
walk with him
along the road
to the pine tree
where he left his guitar,

The whole way
to his truck,
the whole shivering
ride home, me squashed
up against the open window
in case there's still the stench,
he's like: "Are you okay?
I'm sorry, I'm so sorry."

And I can't tell
if he's too sweet,
too grossed out,
or too petrified
to say anything
but "Sorry."

Or if there's any,
any, any way
he doesn't know.

Not that it matters.
I can never
see him again.

Tubes draining stuff out,
dripping stuff in:

Clothespin thingy
on her finger,

Electrodes, wires,
glubs and beeps.

I watch her mom and grandma
play gin rummy

While nurses bustle
and Shannon sleeps.

All night
through the curtain
I hear whispered words
of comfort,
complications,
prayer.

Meanwhile,
I eat
cupcake
after
cupcake
until
somehow
I sleep.

Only to wake
tangled in covers
gunked with frosting,
clammy with sweat,
in a room still dark
and, except for the gurgle
of machines, silent as a tomb.

No. Shannon's breathing.
Don't think. Don't look
at crumpled cupcake papers.
Or my face in the mirror.
Brush my teeth. Wash.
Push the pole up the hall,
down the hall, up again.
Walk yesterday away.

"Something you need?"
The clock on the wall
behind the nurse
says four-thirty-three.

"Food?"

Hunger surges as I say it.
And a calm giddiness
almost like a runner's high.

"Um. Do you think it's possible
to get so mad it blasts
the sickness out of you?"

Knowing full well if that was true
Shannon would be out dancing.
But then why this sudden . . .

"Because I had a giant meltdown
yesterday, and even though I ate
like seven cupcakes last night,
if you gave me a lobster right now,
I'd eat it shell and all.
Plus just yesterday
I could barely walk this far,
and now . . ."

The nurse checks my chart
on her computer.
"You've had four days
of pretty powerful meds.
Some of it might be the steroids
revving you up, but it looks to me
like you're on the mend."

FIFTH DAY

Before the sun,
before the carts,

Before the blood man
comes for blood,

Brisk and chipper,
the shower-cap docs

Crowd round her bed,
nodding as the briskest

Reads out the latest
from her chart,

Frowning when he asks
if she's passed gas,

Striding off again
when she doesn't answer.

Med students' eyes are softer
than the docs'.
They file in
behind their Duck in Chief,
trying to look earnest
when he asks about the gas,

Their eyes so soft
yet so determined
to miss nothing
and fix everything,

These shiny-haired, blue-scrubbed girls
and one cute rumpled guy
who even walks like a duck
and looks like he would kill for coffee.

I can't help wondering how I'd
look in scrubs like theirs,
stethoscope around my neck,
asking how people feel today,

So relieved and proud
when they say "Better."
Which, amazingly, I do.
Because, it seems, I am.

My numbers are looking great,
they say. They're cutting
back the evil juice. Switching me
to pills instead of the IV.

Which makes my heart so glad
so guilty, so scared
when I peek through
at silent Shannon,

Tubes gurgling stuff out,
dripping stuff in,
legs in puffing
life-preserver thingies,

Pain button
in her hand,

I think of calling Mom.
Eat another cupcake.

"So is it true
I'm getting better?"
I ask the Orange Croc Doc.

"What does better mean
for somebody like me?"

Inside my drawer
Mom's cell buzzes,
buzzes.

"It means,"
the Orange Croc Doc says,
when I don't pick it up,
"you're on your way
to being out of here."

"Then what?
Cuz what if I start, like, hoping,
and then—"

The voice mail dings.

"I think you know, Chess,
Crohn's is a tough and
unpredictable disease."

"Yes. Everyone keeps saying that."

"Crohn's can flare up
and it can calm down again.
But let's not get ahead
of ourselves. For now,

the plan is to taper
you off the steroids,
to get you in remission,
and back to your life."

"What if unpredictable doesn't work
for me? What if I need to know
what my life is gonna be?
How do I know I won't . . . what if I . . ."

The text chime rings.

"That's gonna be my mom.
Telling me I upset Nana.
Or Nana telling me I really upset Mom.
It was my birthday yesterday.
I kind of ruined it for everyone."

"Then let's start by making today better,"
she says. "I know you'll be glad
to lose the IV.
How about a shower?
Wash yesterday away.
Put some curl
back in your hair."

Unhooked,
I'm light enough
to float up
to the ceiling,
flutter
to the bathroom floor.

The nurse swaddles
the IV needle
still sticking in my vein
with plastic wrap
and rubber bands,
hands me two big towels.

"Enjoy," she says.

Anyone who thinks heaven
is not hot water
behind a locked door
has forgotten
what it means
to live.

Okay.
Like getting up your nerve

To step
onto the scale, I edge

Zitful, puff-bellied, pin-eyed,
moon-faced, brown-toothed,
crawled-from-the-crypt
seaweed-hair steroid girl?

Or interestingly older,
poet-pale, heart-achingly brave,
winningly fragile, newly wise?
With dragon eyes?

Toward
the mirror.

Hmm.

Face fatter
than I'd like.
Except for the bruisey
circles under my eyes,
cadaver pale.

But clean.
Not fat.
In fact,
really thin.

In fact, somebody
who liked me/
loved me/
really knew me
might,
if they weren't
grossed out or terrified
I might die,
might in the right light,
candles, or maybe
moonlight . . .

Hey, David.
Does ethereal antelope
work for you?

"Text me,"
he said.

Or did he say
anything

as I stumbled
from his car
thanking God
for the dark
so he couldn't see
me cry?

No.
Let it go.
Start by making today better.

I press the call button
beside the toilet.

A nurse voice booms:
"Need some help in there?"

"No. I just wanted to ask.
Does this place
let people
wear clothes?"

In the last pajamas I hope/swear/hope
I will ever wear, here or possibly in life,

I scrunch, twist, twirl my wet hair
to help it curl, step

From the steamy bathroom
into my room's early-morning sun.

So my heart should soar
when Mom, dressed for work, appears
with my gray sweats, a choice of tees,
my underwear, my bra.

Gingerly, as if she's from the bomb
disposal squad, she steps toward me,
lifts a careful eyebrow
at my pajamas.

"I thought you might want something
a little less . . . not that it wasn't really
sweet of Nana, but . . ."

I give her
a matching eye roll,
lift my eyebrow in return.

"You've saved me
from her sushi."

When we need something safe
to bond around, a Nana joke
is tried and true.

"And look at you!
No tubes.
All clean and shiny.
Practically your old self again.
I thought about bringing jeans,
but then I thought, no, better . . ."

And I'm about to thank her

for her perfect timing, step
into her arms, tell her
I didn't mean
to ruin the party,

When she tells me Bri
called last night to say
she and Lexie took a drive
to Sugar Snap Farm
to pick up some raspberries
for my birthday.

And the lava
starts boiling up again.

"What? Mom, I specifically
told you . . ."

Ears buzz
like electrocuted beetles.

"I'm finally
starting to feel a little better,
finally got myself to stop
thinking about things,
and now here you are
telling me my friends
did exactly
what I told you
and told them
not
to do?"

And I can't let myself yell
or I'll wake poor Shannon,

And I hate the hurt
in Mom's eyes as she says,

"I did tell them.
I told them the other day
you're not supposed
to eat anything with seeds."

But still the words howl
out of me:

"AND NOW YOU'RE TELLING ME
I CAN'T EVEN EAT RASPBERRIES?"

"Chessie.
I talked to the doctor.
She said they're going to lower
your steroid dose again tomorrow.
That should help with the mood swings
and there are plenty of things
you *can* eat. She said—"

"DO I LOOK LIKE
I WANT TO HEAR
ABOUT MOOD SWINGS?
I HAVE NO CONTROL
OVER ANYTHING
IN MY LIFE.

NOT MY BODY.
NOT MY FRIENDS.
NOT EVEN YOU."

"**W**e don't take stress, we give
stress, isn't that what you said?"

I tell Shannon through the curtain
when Mom's gone.

"You said it was time to lose
that sorry shit. So I did."

Tell her even
though she's sleeping.

"It's okay to be pissed, right?
Pissed is good.

"Like being pissed at you
if I thought you knew

"You were having that surgery
And didn't tell me."

Then I leave a really pissed message
on Bri's phone.

All day I prowl the halls,
passing every pole-pushing hospital-gowned patient

Trudging up and down like me, nodding
to every thumbs-up smile I pass,

Trying not to look for Bri or Lexie around every corner.
Or think or wonder.

Walk, doze, nose around
the nurses' station.

Try to ignore Mrs. Murch's incessant complaining,
Mom's cell's insistent buzzing from my drawer.

Peer at Shannon through the curtain
as doctors confer, hover.

Listen to her mom and grandma
ask about fevers after surgery,

Tell her we're just waiting
for her new meds to kick in.

Watch them sponge her face,
murmur, pray.

Tweeze my eyebrows.
Turn my TV on to drown out her whimpers.

Turn it off again. Shut down Mom's cell.
Turn off the ringer on the bedside phone.

Talk to an aide
named Ernie.

Take another walk, another nap, fetch nurses
when her IV's beeping or the groans get louder.

"So, Shannon, did you know
everyone here has name tags?
The blood man's Astro.
Orange Croc Doc
is Dr. E. Hochstein.

"And did we know
the shrink guy
is Dr. B. Blank?
Dr. Duck's name
is C. Nguyen.

"The floor clerk, Ms. P. Johnson,
who's worked here thirty-seven years,
showed me a nest with three baby
pigeons peeping so loud
you could hear them
through the kitchen window.

"Did you even know
there was a kitchen room?
Where you can help yourself
to powdered soup and tea?

"And a lounge down the hall
with magazines?
They were all like *Golf Digest*
and *Gastroenterology Today*,

"But I can look
for something better
for you if you want,
when I go out again."

Study myself in the mirror
eavesdrop, pester anyone

who'll talk to me
about complications after surgery,

read *Golf Digest*,
read *Gastroenterology Today*.

"So, Shannon, I thought
you might want to know.
The Orange Croc Doc's 'E'
is for Elina.

"And those pigeons?
I didn't actually hear them peeping.
I was just, you know, trying
to entertain you.

"Okay. Now here's
something entertaining.
My dinner tray.
Want to know what's on it?

"Something that may
have been a veggie
in its former life.
Cream soup the same green
as the curtain.
Rice with flecks of some sort.
Rigor mortis chicken.

"Believe me, Shannon,
you are missing nothing."

Guiltily gobble
every scrap.

"I know, Shannie.
I know it hurts.

"But the thing about pain?
It fades.

"If women could remember
pain, there'd be no babies.

"You'll say what we all say:
It hurt so much

"You could hardly stand
how much.

"It hurt so bad
you thought you'd die.

"But it'll just be words.
Those words will be just ghosts,

And the stories you tell nothing
but stories.

"And you'll jump out of that bed
like you always do,

"Hold your baby
like I'm holding you now,

"And get on with your life,
the same pain in my butt

"You always were
and always will be.

"I promise you.
These days will fade away."

"**A**nd I promise you, too, Chess."
Shannon's grandma's shoes squeak
as she walks around to my side,
the light just bright enough
for me to read
East Greenbush Wrestling
in peeling letters on her hoodie.

"Now let me just tuck you in
and say sleep tight.
Good night to you too, Mrs. Murch,"
she calls through the curtain.

"Hmmph!" snorts Mrs. Murch.
"I can tell you're a nurse
by the way you wake me up
to say good night."

I think
about calling Mom
to say good night,
another sorry.

Find Bri's text waiting
on Mom's cell in the drawer.

Why r u so mad???
We barely talked to D
just told him ur up in Albany
in the hospital really sick.
That's all we said besides
how r the razberries today ☺
He looked a little weird/not glad
to see us. Then he rushed off so we
couldn't ask anything even if
we wanted. R u ever
gonna tell us wassup?

Someone in the hall guffaws.
Farts like a fourth-grade
farting contest echo
through the wall.

Not even a whimper
breaks Shannon's silence.

How can I be so mad when
my little drama, my little life
feels a zillion miles away?

"Why is she so quiet?" I ask the nurse
who hangs another IV bag for Shannon.

"She had a tough day."

"But it's a good sign, right?
That she's stopped moaning?"

He puts a finger to his lips.
"It's past midnight, lovey.
Go to sleep."

"I thought the thing
about being young is that—
except for, like, can I run
a half marathon,
am I as cute as so-and-so,
is my butt too big for these jeans—
you don't have to think
about your body.

"You're not supposed
to have to worry if
it's gonna make it
through the day.

"That's one of the things
making me so mad.
Not just for me.
For you.

"Sometimes it feels like
mad's the only thing we've got
to get us through.

"Shannon?
You're still mad, right?"

I listen for her breath.

Hear nothing
but the puff of her machines,
Mrs. Murch's gargley snores.

"Shannon?
Now you're scaring me."

"That she's not answering
doesn't mean she's not hearing, right?"
I ask the nurse when he tiptoes in again
to check our vitals.

"Why are you still up?" he asks.
"It's four a.m."

I count my breaths,
her breaths,
Mrs. Murch's snores.

The night beetles
swarm.

When I pull back
the curtain, I see

covers tight as
her grandma tucked her.

Melting ice chips
in her cup.

Face turned
to the wall.

To the hum of her machines
I sing us choir songs,
list favorite movies of all time,
Baskin-Robbins flavors,
brands of cereal,

Boys I liked, loved,
wished I dated, hated;
books, games, dog names
if we had a dog;
Crayola colors.

And I know
if I keep talking
I can keep her going:

"Inch worm,
Bittersweet,
Tumbleweed,
Fern.
Cerulean,
Cerise,
Sepia,
Mango Tango.

"Atomic Tangerine,
Wild Watermelon,
Dandelion,
Neon Carrot,
Timberwolf,
Mauvelous . . ."

"**S**hannon?

"You're not like in a coma or something,
are you?

"Cuz my theory is
you're not talking cuz
you're like, 'What'd I do
to deserve this shit?
I'm sick of it.
Wake me when it's over.'

"That's how I feel, too.

"Shannon, if I tell you what happened
to me on the island
will you promise not to tell?

"Shannon?
Did you hear
what I just told you?

"Blink once
for *Yes*

"Twice
for *Fuck You.*

"Shannon.
Talk to me."

SIXTH DAY

Early as yesterday,
brisk and chipper,
the surgeons whip closed
her curtain.

"How we doing today, Ms. Williams?
Mind if we take a look at the incision?

"Good. I see your fever's down."

"Excuse me. I'm a little worried
about her," I call out, same
as I've told the nurse each time
he checks our vitals.

"We've got your infection under
control. How's the pain,
Ms. Williams?
Passed any gas?"

"I'm worried about Shannon."

I catch the eye of Dr. Nguyen
as the duck brigade arrives,

Listen to the head duck tell
Mrs. Murch, "Great news!
You're going home!"

Listen to her complain she's still
a very sick woman,

Listen as they reel off
Shannon's numbers,

Listen to the head duck
asking if by any chance
she's passed gas from below.

"It's not something to be shy about,
Ms. Williams.
Passing gas is a good thing.
Passing gas means your guts
are waking up, so we can start
you on some food, begin—"

"Doctor!
Forget the gas!
I'm worried she's not talking!"

I wait to be shushed,
soothed, scolded.

Instead, I hear a croak
rusty as Mrs. Klein:

"You better hope you're not here
when I pass gas, Doc.

"If you are, get ready to run.

"When I pass gas
this whole fuckin' hospital's
gonna go up in flames."

Dr. Nguyen takes a quick detour
past my bed.

"I think your friend's gonna be okay."

He's trying not to smile.

"She's back!"
I tell Astro, the blood man,
Bobby, the vitals guy.

"Watch out, Shannon's back!"
I warn Dr. R. Schmidt, the doc she
    advised
to be a coroner, Joyce, the nurse
who calls us cookie.

A croak, a cough, a rough clearing
of her throat:

"Yo. Cookie! That you?
What day of the week is it?
And if you tell me the first day
of the rest of my life, I might have to—"

"She's back, all right."
Joyce shakes her head,
smiles, handing me my pills.
"It's Tuesday, Shannon.
Good to hear your cheery voice again."

"What's good is having that damn
tube outta my nose.
You could get that pain pump thing
outta here, too."

"You sure?
You're a brave little girl, Shannon.
You don't need to be a hero."

I follow Joyce around

to Shannon's side,
throat full
with words
that even in my ears
sound puny, lame.

Arms tight around her pillow,
pain button in her hand
Shannon is sleeping.

Crisp in her lab coat,
curls tamed with pins,
Dr. Hochstein—who in my mind
will always be the Orange Croc Doc—
pulls up a plastic chair
across from Mom and me.

"So, Chess? Ready
to go home tomorrow?"

I'm grateful we're in the lounge
so Shannon can't see my joy.

"Excellent. Because . . ."

But if I'm so happy,
why do I hear myself add
"I guess?"

Why am I watching
branches bang
against the windows,
people shaking out umbrellas,

When I should be listening
to her tell us how many books,
blogs, sites, support groups
are available
for teens like me;

How many drugs
to put me in remission,
and with luck keep me there,
with new ones all the time;

While Mom, with the same careful smile
on her face I feel on mine,
takes notes,
talks prescriptions,
doctor appointments,
food restrictions.

"Any questions, Chess?"

Besides: Will Shannon
ever be okay?

Besides: How do I know when I look at Shannon
I'm not seeing Future Me?

Besides: How do you not hate your friends
for being well?

Your mom for not making it all
just go away?

Besides: How do you know who you are
when you can't trust your own body?

How do you act when you're so mad,
so scared of what's inside?

"Chess." The Orange Croc Doc
takes her glasses off,
leans closer.

"You've been pretty sick
Probably for a long time."

I watch a leaf
shaped like a mitten
stick to the window glass.

"And this is a lot for you
to swallow."

Watch the parking-lot gate
swing open for a car,
drop down.

Remember the brain-frying tiredness,
the pain endured
to get through a day,

The terrifying pains
that night . . .

I look at Mom,
look away.

"Sometimes
I thought
I might be
dying.

"But I didn't
say anything
because . . ."

An ache
worse than tears
cinches my throat.

"I thought it was something I did,
or didn't do, or should have done better,
something I ate, or my period,
or stress.

"Thinking I could fix it
with, like, vitamins, or coffee, or cardio,
or cutting out carbs, or running so fast
I could outrun *it* . . .
which sounds pretty stupid now,

"But it just feels like all these folks—
at school, at colleges
I haven't even applied to yet,
not to mention you, Mom . . ."

I count squares on the floor.

"Are counting on me
to be perfect."

Mom fumbles for a tissue.

A raindrop slides down
the windowpane.

"Plus, I'm like you, Mom.
I thought if I didn't say anything,
it would go away.

"Even now.
After all this,
I just want to believe . . .

make believe
it's not there."

"You know what, Chess?"
The Orange Croc Doc leans closer still.
"When you're in remission,
you may not have to make believe.
You may not notice
any symptoms at all.

"And, Chess, we may not know for certain
what triggers this disease,
but one thing's for sure:
It's nothing
you did
or didn't do."

Mom blows her nose.

"And another thing,"
my Orange Croc Doc says
as we all stand to go.
"The upside
of these autoimmune diseases?
Most of the time, you look just fine.

"Which can be a drag
if you're looking for sympathy,
but it means you can decide
how much you want to say.
To whom. And when."

"And can I run again?"

"Why not?
You may have to take it easy
for now. Start out slow.
But yes. Go for it!
Go back to your life.
Do everything
you can sensibly do."

"But how will I know?"

"Chess.
You're not in this alone."

Mom's nodding,
nodding.
Nodding.

Slower than the doc
texting as he walks,

Slower than the squashed-hair lady
in her bunny slippers,

Slower than the guy trying to keeping his gown
from flapping open while he trudges with his pole,

Silently, holding hands,
Mom and I tromp the hall.

"Oh, my goodness!

Mom drops my hand,
stops walking.

"I totally forgot . . ."

Digs from her purse
a padded envelope.

"This was left for you
at the nurses' station
this morning."

Inside, with a note
rubber-banded around it,
is my phone.

For an instant I'm back
on the island,
in his arms,
in a swoon
of such
deliciousness . . .

"Excuse me, sugar."
A cart piled high with dishes
pulls up beside us.

"You didn't fill out your menu
for tomorrow," says the meal lady.

Till the spasms,
the stink,
the . . .

And yet
he drove
an hour
to Albany
to bring me this.

She hands me a stubby pencil.

"I won't be here tomorrow."

"But you'll be here for breakfast.
And by the time they get your discharge
sent up, you might be wanting lunch."

cold cereal

   hot meat loaf sandwich

cream of broccoli

     cream of wheat

Words dance before my eyes.

"No dessert, hon?
We've got apple pie."

And now why is Mrs. Murch here,
asking if she can get some breakfast.
Anything will do. Her son-in-law
was supposed to be here hours ago.
He's never late, and by the way,
wasn't Mom in her English class?
She never forgets a face. Oh, and . . .

"I don't think so," Mom says.
"I went to school in Colonie.
We were just headed to the bathroom.
So if you'll excuse us, Mrs. Murch . . ."

She gives me her Nana eyebrow,
whispers: "Meet you
back in the room.
Go read your note."

So lucky   still on the rock

          crevicey thing

  even so

     battery

     vacuum cleaner   noodle
dessicant

        bag of rice   rotate

    to you sooner if

My eyes race
past the words
to his P.S.:

Anyway. It seems to be OK now.
Hope you're OK too.
David

To his P.P.S.:

Did I ever thank you for
  remembering the guitar?? The
  way it rained
that night it would have been deader
  than the phone.

To the wings
he's drawn
around his number.

Heart galloping,
I boot up the phone.

Thumbs bumbling,
type the numbers.

Read, reread his note.
What to say
to match his tone?

Thanks.

Too dry?
Or is dry good?
Did I hit send too soon?

I'm much better, thanks!
Getting out tomorrow!

Two texts,
two exclamation points,
too eager?
Like I'm hinting
I want to see him?

Do I?

In the mirror,
skin blue as skim milk,
hands purply
with IV bruises,
bloated belly,
jutting collarbones.

And yet . . .

"Chess?"

Mom's knocking
on the bathroom door.
"You've been in there a long time."

"I'm—"

The text chime rings.

**Wasn't sure u'd want to see anyone
so I just dropped it at the desk.**

That was so nice of u.

**I was kinda worried about it
so went to look the next day
and put back the canoe we hijacked** ☺
Got yr jacket too, btw.

"Chessie? Sweetie?"

U swam out there?

Duh.

"I'm okay, Mom.
You don't have to stand outside the door.
How 'bout I meet you in the room?"

**Was with my dad all weekend.
I told u he lives near the lake.**

0, right.

He thought i couldn't fix it.
The noodle dessicant did it.

What's noodle dessicant?

How long
can we keep talking
about the phone?

I know I already said
sorry about that night but
at least I got yr phone working again.

He knows.
He has to know.

u don't have to be sorry.
It wasn't u it wasn't me.
I seem to have a disease.

No reply.

Night beetles
begin to fly.

David don't worry. U can't catch it. ☺☹

☺ **and if ur getting out u must be ok**
but why didn't yr friends
   say something to me
besides u were in the hospital and

giving me looks like i was some kind of
evil demon.

I told them not to talk to u.
Didn't want anyone to know.

My cell rings.

"Listen," he says.
"I never say stuff like 'be there for you,'
but how can your friends be there for you
if they don't know what's going on?"

"Friend?"
The word
prickles in my nose,
mists my eyes.

"Hello?
Chess, you there?"

I nod
as if he can see.

"I was a little worried, you know.
I mean . . . it's not exactly
what I had in mind
for the night."

Before Monitor Me
can stop me, I'm saying:

"You know what
my friend Shannon
would say to that?
No shit!"

"**S**o my friend David?
Who I was with that night?
Who fixed my phone?"

I feel the heat of Mom's wanting
to know everything fighting
her not wanting to screw up
what we've started.

And though all I want
is to climb under the covers,
replay the good parts,
delete the bad parts, maybe cry,
I perch on her chair arm,
rest my head on her shoulder.

She scoots over
to make room in the chair,
lifts an arm around me.
I nestle down beside her.

"He lives in Hillsdale, Mom.
And he's working at Sugar Snap Farm
for a year so he can save enough
for college. He's really smart, Mom.
And really nice.
And I don't know when yet, but
I'm pretty sure
I'm gonna see him.

"And I need you to know.
What everyone thought
happened that night?

It wasn't what happened."

"I know.
I found the dress in the trash.
I washed it.
Don't worry, Chess.
It came out fine."

"When I give it back to Lexie
do I have to tell her?"

"You don't have to tell anyone anything
you're not ready to tell."

So . . . if I don't feel like talking to anyone
for a while?"

Her arm tightens
around me.

"It's okay."

"It sucks being sick."

"Truly," she says.

I nod
into her armpit.

Keep on
nodding.

"**Y**O!
NO CRYING HERE!"

"Oh. Sorry, Shannon.
Did I wake you?"

"And what'd I tell you
about that sorry shit?

"You're not sorry.
You told me yourself.
You're pissed as hell.
Like me."

"So I was right! You did hear
what I told you in the night!"

"Yeah. Now you gonna open
that curtain and
tell me what I've missed
these past two days,
or what?"

"So . . . did you hear
the other stuff?

"The gross stuff?
About what happened?"

"Yeah. Bummer."

227

"Well, I just talked to him.
He knows, Shannon.
He saw.
And I think he still
wants to be with me."

Many texts,
some chats,
plans made,
a lot of laps,
bad food,
a nap.

A tube removed,
some hobbling
bathroom walks,
some sitting up,
a lot of naps.

Sweet dreams
of going home.

"**S**hannon? Y'awake?

"Listen. I don't want you
to be disappointed
if he's not, like, movie-star hot
or outwardly amazing."

"Who're you telling?
I'm not the one in *luuvv* and shit.
I'm not even gonna see the dude."

"To someone who doesn't know
him, he might be kind of gawky.
Possibly a little geeky."

"Geekier than you?"

"But with the warmest, darkest eyes.
Hair the color of caramel,
that like curls down around—"

"So you're saying
you're in geek lust."

"Yes. No.
I don't know.
No. It's way more."

"You really think you meet
some boy and . . . boom!
The world is beautiful!
Your trouble's gone!

"No. No. I know.
But . . ."

It ain't like that.
Except in songs."

"So, besides the famous Anthony
Morabito, you never fell in love
at first sight?"

"Only with my daughter."

"What about her father?"

A noise like air whooshing
out of a balloon.

"So you wanna see her picture?"
Holding her belly, wincing
with each step,

She hobbles to my side.

On her phone, I see
Joya sprawled on an afghan,
in felt antlers;

In a Valentine's Day onesie.
grinning in a baby bouncer;

Running through a sprinkler,
mischief in her eyes;

In the plump arms
of a smiling red-haired lady.

"Oh wow. She looks
like you.
She's beautiful.

"Your other grandmother
looks nice, too."

I sound
so lame.

"Here's me.
I told you I was hot, right?"

Shannon, prom queen shiny
in a silver, slitted strapless gown
stiletto sandals;

Shannon, mugging for the camera,
giant sunglasses,
ginormous hoop earrings;

Shannon, in a black puffer,
animal-print leggings,
on the steps of a white ranch house
with green shutters.

"Yeah, I don't live in a trailer anymore,
case you were wondering.
We've lived here since we left my dad.

"Who won't be drunk or
back here, I'm guessing
till next weekend,
when you're long gone.
Case you were worried."

There's so much
I want to ask, say, but
I don't want to stop
her talking, so
I thumb to the next picture:

Shannon leaning into
a buff, buzz-haired, smiling guy
in an army uniform,

Red-and-blue striped tee
stretched tight
over her belly,

No hint of sick
or dragon
in her eyes.

"Yeah. I didn't need
to think about being sick then.
Look at me: I had it so in control.

"And he was all patting my belly
and shit about being a father.
Till I stopped taking my meds.
Which I already knew was a bad idea

"Cuz I was already kinda flaring
even on the meds, but
I didn't want anything
messing up my baby.

"So my mom'd fill the prescriptions
and I'd flush 'em. Lie.
And for a while,
even when it got bad again,

"I didn't miss one day of school,
showed up for my job
at the vet clinic every Saturday,
telling myself

"It wasn't the Crohn's,
just being pregnant. Cuz I read
Crohn's takes a time-out sometimes
when you're pregnant.

"Except the only time-out I got
was in the damn hospital.
On the damn tubes
and evil juice again.

"Which, as you can see
from the pictures,
didn't mess up Joya,
thank God, but . . .

"TMI, right?

"Only reason I'm telling
you is so if you ever think
about stopping your meds,
no matter how much you hate
taking them, you'll think of me
and know
it's the dumbest
stupidest,
most asinine
thing you could do."

"Chess? You still awake?"

"Yeah."

"Whatcha doing?"

"Lying here.
Staring at the ceiling."

"Before?
When I said
I didn't care
about Joya's father?"

"Yeah.
I know."

"Chess? What time is it?"

"Twenty past three."

"I could use a bowl of that
ice cream around now."

"Me too."

SEVENTH DAY

"Look at you,
all dressed and ready to go
before they've even come
to draw your blood. That's one thing
you won't miss, I know!"

Celandine, the night aide, smiles
as she takes my very last vitals.

"You better tell your mom to feed you up.
That or buy you smaller pants.

"And how you doing, Miss Shannon?
Looks like you're getting some of
the old sparkle in your eye."

"Still here. Still me.
Don't ask
About the gas."

"I don't wanna hear the G-word,"
she warns the surgeons.

"And don't tell me it's Job One,"
she tells the duck brigade.
"I got my daughter to get back,
my GED, get my ass to college
so I can be a doctor
like you guys, only better."

"It's fuckin' gas.
It's passed before,
it'll pass again."

"**H**ey. I hear someone's leaving us,"
says Dr. Nguyen on his way out.

"Bet you can't wait
To kiss this place good-bye."

Shannon turns her TV on.

Even through the curtain
I can feel her eyes.

"Is it weird to hug your
doctor?" I ask the Orange Croc Doc
when she officially declares me
good to go.

With a "Hmmph!"
worthy of Mrs. Murch
as she trudges to the bathroom,
Shannon tells her IV pole,
"Next she's gonna be talking
about hugging me."

"Don't bring my lunch.
I'm outta here," I tell the lady
who comes to take away
my breakfast tray.

"The only reason I'm still here is
my mom has to stop by her office

before she can drive up
to get me."

Shannon turns her TV louder.

"I won't be needing that,"
I tell Green Jacket Man
when he parks a wheelchair
beside my bed.

"Thank you for taking such good care
of my trash," I tell the cleaning man.
"I'm leaving today.
I'm going—"

"YO! NEWSFLASH, CUPCAKE!
WE KNOW THAT! EVERYONE
IN THIS HOSPITAL
KNOWS THAT!

"WANT ME TO RENT THE
GOODYEAR BLIMP
SO THE WHOLE WORLD
WILL KNOW?"

A few laps
around the nurses' station.

Check my phone.

Think about texting
Bri or Lexie.

Decide it might feel easier
when I get home.

Inspect myself
in the bathroom mirror.

How many times
can one person pee?

Check my phone.

Try on my other sweats,
the other tops,
twist my hair up,
braid tiny braids,
try to tie my hair back
with my hospital bracelet,
which I probably should not
have bit, sawed, nipped
with my nail clippers,
because now some alarm
might go off
when I try to leave.

"Shannon. Why does my hair look so bad?
It looked so good yesterday.

"These pants are so baggy!
Like I've got on, like, Pampers ..."

Her TV's blasting now.

I yank open the curtain.

I grab her clicker.
Kill the sound.

"HEY!
WHAT ARE YOU DOING?"

"Shannon. I don't mean
to be annoying you."

"Yeah? Well, you're like the dogs
in our kennel, pacing in their cages,
ears up, tongues dangling, butts
  wiggling.
I'm surprised you don't bark
anytime anyone goes past!
It's setting off my evil juice!"

"I'm setting off my
evil juice. Sorry."

"And what'd I tell you
about apologizing!"

"How 'bout
'We don't take stress,
we give stress'?"

"Yeah, well,
don't give your stress to me!

"Yeah. Hey. It's Shannon,"
she calls into the intercom.
"Could somebody please
come in here and unhook me?"

"Where you going?"

"For a walk.
"I'm supposed to be walking.
So I'm taking a walk."

"What if Mom comes
and you're not here?
No. Never mind.
No worries. Go ahead.
We'll find you."

"For what?"

"So you and I can . . .
you know . . ."

"Are you not hearing me?
For what? A month from now
we could pass each other
on the street and never know.

"And don't gimme some shit about
how sorry you are to be leaving.
Cuz if it was me?

And I was leaving you here?
I'd be like, 'Bye!'"

"Yes. And I'd get it.
Because we're friends, you and me.
And you're not just my friend, okay?
What Joyce, the nurse, said yesterday?
About don't be a hero?
I don't mean this to sound cheesy,
but you really are my—"

"YO! NURSE! KELLIANNE!
ARE WE WALKING, OR WHAT?"

I can't remember
feeling this glad
to see my mom
since the first week
of preschool.

"Excuse me."

We're just gathering up my bags
when Kellianne walks through the door.

"Shannon said don't wait.
She said something might be . . . you know . . ."

Comes closer,
drops to a half whisper:

"About to happen. Gas-wise.

"She thought it might not be that cool
for you if she stuck around.

"Oh, wait! That's her,
buzzing me now!"

"Do not hug me.
I don't do huggy."

"Too bad." I hold on
till Shannon's arms
tighten around me.

When she lets go,
in purple pen I scribble
my contact info on her hand,

Dragon-eye her right back
as I pass the pen to her.
"Now I need yours."

As Mom rolls
my unnecessary mandatory wheelchair
toward the elevator,
I hear:

"Do I need that brave little 'you're my hero' shit?
A, I may be short, but I am not little.
B, no brave about it. You do what you do
and you get through.
Which I will do.

"Now Job One's done,
it's time to get myself cute again,
get my driver's license,
get my daughter home with me . . .

"And how's she expect me to call her
when she can't even write the numbers
so you can read 'em?

"Hey, Kellianne,
Is that a four or a nine?"

AFTER

In starry dark a girl
sings while a boy
strums his guitar.

Her new running shoes flash
as they jog through
coppery October light.

In a booth
close to the bathroom
in an old Chinese restaurant

Two girls share
pistachio ice cream
with a little girl here for the holidays.

ACKNOWLEDGMENTS

This book has been a long journey. I have many people to thank:

Theresa Nelson, Susan Patron, and Virginia Walters, for believing in The Girls from the beginning, for patiently reading and rereading, cheering me on, and putting up with what must have seemed like endless whining.

Deborah Heiligman, Patricia Lakin Koenigsberg, Elizabeth Levy, Roxane Orgill, and Erika Tamar, for their sustaining friendship, brilliant suggestions, and fine editing skills these many years.

Phyllis Reynolds Naylor, for creating the PEN/Phyllis Naylor Working Writer Fellowship, and for her warmth and enthusiasm when The Girls received the award.

My editor, Anne Schwartz, for believing that the early pages she saw could be a book, and then, with tenacity and great good humor, urging it into being and making it more than I'd dreamed. Stephanie Pitts, for her enormous care with the manuscript from beginning to end.

I must also thank Richard Jackson, from whom I've learned so much, so happily.

Chess and Shannon's story is entirely fiction, but I've tried my best to get the medical details right and to accurately present what is known about Crohn's disease at this time. For that, and so much else, I thank Dr. Scott Weber.

There are no words for my gratitude to my husband, Peter Frank, for his incomparable editor's eye and for encouraging, inspiring, and sticking with me. Through everything.

ABOUT THE AUTHOR

Lucy Frank won a PEN/Phyllis Naylor Working Writer Fellowship for her work on *Two Girls Staring at the Ceiling*. The author of eight novels for young adults and middle graders, she divides her time between New York City and upstate New York. Learn more at lucyfrank.com.